Amy's Gold

ii

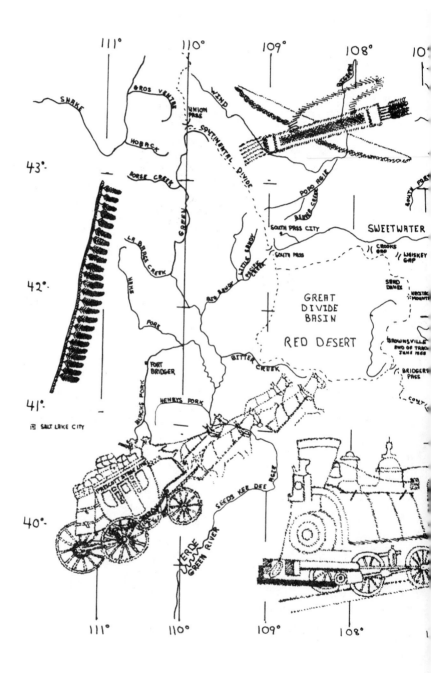

iv

Western wind, when wilt thou blow,
The small rain down can rain?
Christ, if my love were in my arms,
And I in my bed again!

anonymous
Middle Ages

Amy's Gold

a novel by

Robert O. Burgess

Best Wishes,
Robert O Burgess

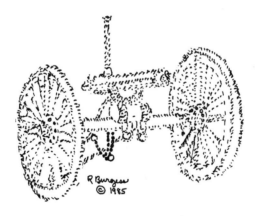

WITH ILLUSTRATIONS BY THE AUTHOR

SWEETWATER PRESS
LARAMIE

AMY'S GOLD: A NOVEL

FIRST EDITION – 1985

For information address:
SWEETWATER PRESS
1071 Duna Drive
Laramie, WY 82070

Library of Congress Catalog Number: 85-62546
ISBN: 0-9615504-0-6
Typesetting: Betty Doerges (Betty's Desk)
Printed In The United States of America

ABOUT THE AUTHOR

Robert O. Burgess was born in Carl Junction, Missouri, in 1934. The University of Oregon conferred the Doctor of Medicine degree to him in 1964. He attended Colorado State College of Education and the University of Wyoming. He received the Bachelor of Science degree from the University of Oregon. He served four years as a Hospital Corpsman in the United States Navy, the last two years with the Marine Corps in Okinawa. For the past twenty years Doctor Burgess has practiced medicine in Laramie, Wyoming.

DEDICATED

To my son Mark, who rode horseback with me up the Hoback River, Granite Creek, Swift Creek, and over the top to the headwaters of the Gros Ventre River. To my daughter Brenda, who rode her horse, Cloudy, along Gold Creek near South Pass. And to my wife Edna, who sat with me high above the beautiful canyon that was South Pass City.

AUTHOR'S PREFACE

Over the past eighteen years I had taken an annual extended trip to the headwaters of a different river in Wyoming's magnificent mountains. The use of the pack horse and mule was the way to enter those high alpine passes where snow-fields had watered patches of wild strawberries. Many years ago the theme of this novel germinated along the banks of the Seeds-kee-dee Agia. Initially, Amy's story was to be strictly fiction, but as the panorama of the setting unfolded, it became increasingly important to me to explain the evolution of the land and its people.

Prior to 1868 powerful events led to the building of the Union Pacific Railroad and its western counterpart, the Central Pacific. A narrow, one-hundred-mile strip of Wyoming was the corridor for tens of thousands of adventurous men and women who had traveled West. The early explorers, in the 1820's, were trappers, hunters who carried flint-lock rifles of Leman and Hawken vintage. Twenty years had passed and during the mid-1840's those same mountain men had guided emigrants along the North Platte River. But they had entered Indian lands where Sioux, Cheyenne, Crow, Blackfeet, Shoshone and Arapaho had grown increasingly wary.

Amy would arrive in 1868.

ROB
Laramie
1985

ACKNOWLEDGEMENTS

I wish to thank Ruth Stoll for reading the manuscript and for her encouragement. My thanks to Emmett Chisum of the University of Wyoming, William Robertson Coe Library, for introducing me to Brownsville through a portfolio of publications, letters and records. Several years ago Dr. Paul McGrew, Emeritus Professor of Paleontology, University of Wyoming, told me of his retracing of the steps of James Clyman along the Sweetwater River. When Dr. McGrew learned of my interest in the early beaver hunters, he loaned me his copy of **James Clyman, Frontiersman.** I wish to thank Calvin Lundberg who had done extensive research in the Red Desert regarding grass species in the Great Divide Basin; and the late Dr. S.H. Knight, Head of the Department of Geology, University of Wyoming, my next door neighbor and friend of many years' duration, who took the time to show me spectrograms of prehistoric eggs deposited along the Green River during the Early Eocene.

ROB
Laramie
1985

CONTENTS

CONTENTS

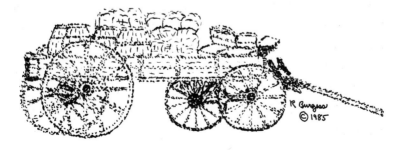

ILLUSTRATIONS
By the Author

Philadelphia Deringer

CHAPTER ONE

1825

The leaves of the aspen had turned to gold early that fall. Along the banks of the river geese fed on ripe currant berries while overhead large flocks of ducks winged their way south in an early migration. Deep snows blocked mountain passes to the northwest while stout horses and tough mules plowded heavy packs and determined men deeper into the wilderness.

"Crow Indian country, Jimmy. Absaroka's. There's no better place. North of South Pass, those mountains just keep getting taller. Buffalo, elk, deer, bear, mountain sheep, beaver and Indians. Good Lord, in that one mountain range a man can run across Gros Ventre, Blackfeet, Arapaho, Sioux, Cheyenne and Shoshone." Henry Robineaux paused to fill his pipe, looked at his ten-year-old son and continued, "I met your mother there."

Jimmy Lee Robineaux, his eyes sparkling with excitement said, "Tell me about the bear, father."

"You mean old Hugh Glass. Well, he was scalped and ripped up bad. It was an old sow griz. Hugh stumbled into her cubs and before he knew it she had his head in her mouth. He didn't get off a shot. We heard his screams, but didn't get there in time. He was about dead, but the captain ordered Jim Bridger and John Fitzgerald to stay and bury him." He stopped talking, knowing the boy would ask for more even though he had heard the story many times before.

"Then what happened, father?"

"Well, that tough old mountain man crawled out of his grave and walked to our fort at the mouth of the Bighorn. Took him several weeks to get there. That happened two years before you were born. Hugh Glass was killed about two years ago by the same 'Rees that were all around us in 1823." He took a long draw on his pipe. "We'll go into the Absaroka's this spring and we'll ride up the Sweetwater, cross South Pass and then along the western edge of the Wind River Mountains. From there we have a choice of either taking the Hoback into Jackson Hole or go north over Union Pass."

I, Jimmy Robineaux, had heard those stories told by other mountain men, but during that winter so many years ago my father made them live. Today, they call that stretch of the Sweetwater the Oregon Trail, but that was long before emigrants could dream of fertile valleys along the Willamette. In those days that was Sublette's Trail. Bridger had ridden it. So had Jedediah Smith, James Clyman, Tom Fitzpatrick, David Jackson, Moses Harris and many, many more mountain men. My father had traveled up the Missouri with them in 1823.

When I was ten years old, in 1835, we camped just outside Fort William on Laramie Fork. We call it Fort Laramie now, where the Laramie River empties into the Platte. That post, built by William Sublette in 1834, stood astride the western movement of a restless nation. But until that time Sublette, Fitzpatrick and Clyman were the men who had traveled it most. In 1826, after Smith, Jackson and Sublette had bought out William Ashley's interest in his fur company, the practice of annual trips to re-supply the fur trappers had become a tradition. Every year over a period of about ten years, the Platte and its western tributary, the Sweetwater, became the lifeblood of Sublette's packtrains to the beaver country.

Ashley was to supply hunting provisions to Smith, Jackson and Sublette for their 1827 hunt, provided they notified him by March 1st in St. Louis. Along the upper reaches of the Sweetwater near South Pass, the December snows were heavy. Jedediah Smith, the explorer of the partnership, was in California. David Jackson had stayed in winter quarters to the west of South Pass to arrange the spring hunt. On January 1st William Sublette and Moses (Black) Harris had set out on snowshoes accompanied by one pack dog. St. Louis, over fourteen hundred miles to the east, was their goal; fifty-nine days their limit. Two weeks out of Ham's Fork near Independence Rock on the Sweetwater, they found buffalo and deep snow drifts. On down the Platte in the middle of what's now Nebraska, nearly starved, sick with exhaustion and still hundreds of miles from civilization, they ate the pack dog. Their strength replenished and small game more abundant, they limped into St. Louis on March 4, 1827, three days overdue. Even so, Ashley honored the contract. Sublette, his mules loaded with traps, guns, lead, powder, shot, blankets, whiskey, sugar and coffee, headed back up the Platte after only ten days' rest.

I had been afoot in those mountains many times, but not by choice. "If you want to keep your hair, you adapt." The Crow Indians' favorite sport was horse stealing. They had run off William Clark's horses in 1805, and Robert Stuart's horses in 1812 after Stuart had led the Astorian's, a party of seven, back from the mouth of the Columbia River where it empties into the Pacific Ocean. Stuart's party traveled east through South Pass, probably the first white men through that gap. Stuart hadn't publicised his important route, and the government seemed unaware of it even though there had been a story in a St. Louis paper that wagons could cross by Stuart's route, South Pass.

Sublette and Smith had been told by the Crow of a pass south of the Popo Agie after they had been unable to cross Union Pass, snowbound during the mid-winter of 1824. It had been just as cold farther south with high winds and driving snows their constant companions. After they had found South Pass on the Sweetwater, they continued west to cross the Big Sandy, and followed it down to the Green River. Then it was March and time for the spring hunt. Jedediah Smith divided the eleven men into two parties with Tom Fitzpatrick and James Clyman leading one group. Sublette was probably with Smith.

Later Tom Fitzpatrick and James Clyman had fallen in with a small band of Shoshone Indians at the confluence of a small stream and the Green River, whose banks were covered with deep grass and a little snow. Beaver meat was the staple diet for both Indian and white man, and early one morning, when the snows were gone, Fitzpatrick, while preparing breakfast, noticed the Indians were gone and so were the horses. He named the stream Horse Creek. After a long walk, they got their horses back, by taking them away from the same bunch of Indians. Likely as not they were my relatives.

Other than by Stuart, the lower Sweetwater hadn't been explored, at least not by white men. Fitzpatrick and Clyman rode down the open banks of the shallow Sweetwater for several miles. Simultaneously Fitzpatrick left Clyman afoot and returned for the rest of the party. James Clyman walked down the Sweetwater to where it joined the Platte from the South. He built a crude shelter in the willows overlooking the river and awaited his friends. He hadn't even struck a fire when he saw the river bank swarming with Indians.

The following day the Indians left the site and Clyman walked on down the river to where it passed through a narrow, rocky gorge, Devil's Gate. Unbeknown to Clyman, Jedediah Smith at that same time had found his camp, and after a long search, had gone back upriver. Clyman remained in the rocks above the Sweetwater for eleven days, and after counting his limited supply of powder and ball, headed for civilization. Before he could arrive, a band of Pawnees had stolen his rifle, knife and powder, but spared his life. Civilization was Ft. Atkinson. Not knowing whether he was on the Platte River or the Arkansas, he had walked over a thousand miles to where the Platte empties into the Missouri River. Well, like I say, those old boys were mountain men!

Ten days later Fitzpatrick and two others also walked into Fort Atkinson and told their story. Fitzpatrick had built a bullboat with willows for the frame which he covered with buffalo skins. When they tried to negotiate Devil's Gate, the boat capsized sending their rifles and packs of fur to the bottom. After retrieving their furs and drying them, they carried them down river to a huge, bare, gray rock, Independence Rock, where they cached their packs. The date was the Fourth of July, 1824.

Fitzpatrick had no more than caught his breath at Fort Atkinson before he was back up the Platte to retrieve their furs, the first pack of commercial goods to come out of Wyoming Territory.

William Ashley now knew the way to the Green River or Seeds-kee-dee Agia as the Indians called it, and in the late fall of 1824 he led a party to Fort Atkinson. While Ashley knew of Fitzpatrick's and Clyman's journey from South Pass down the Sweetwater, thence down the Platte, he did not follow their historic lead. With twenty-five men, including both Fitzpatrick and Clyman and fifty pack horses, they rode up the Platte to the fork of the South Platte, and then up that river to camp at the Cache-la-Poudre River. Then they pack-trained into the Laramie Plains along the eastern edge of the Medicine Bow Range and Elk Mountain. Ashley then led his

band through what would later become known as Bridger's
Pass long before Bridger had found it.

   Now all of that was taking place during 1825, the year
Jimmy Lee Robineaux, raconteur, was born.
   The narrative that follows, is, like Jimmy, fiction. The lure
of gold has intrigued men and women for centuries. It
still does.

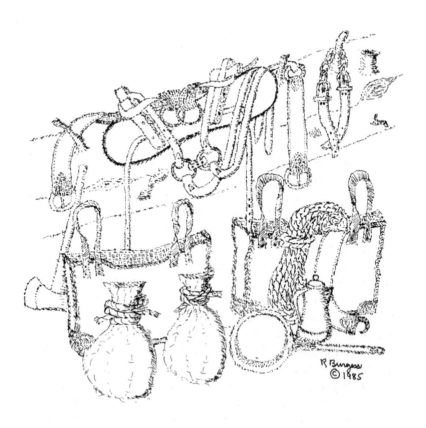

CHAPTER TWO

RED DESERT

During the Early Middle Eocene, fifty million years ago, Lake Gosiute was drying up. Its eastern border, located a few miles to the west of the Red Desert on the western slope of the Continental Divide was home to numerous crocodiles, turtles, flamingos and small dog-sized horses such as *Hyracotherium* with four toes on its front feet and three toes on its back feet. The most numerous fish in Lake Gosiute was *Knightia*, a small herring-like fish. Rushes and reeds were lake-shore plants and palm trees grew in her sandy soil. Cypress, fig, willow and laurel adorned the lower reaches of the lake while oak, maple and beech grew nearby. On the higher slopes fir, spruce and pine grew then as they do today.

Ham's Fork, the Green and Big Sandy Rivers now flow through the ancient bed of Lake Gosiute. Subsequently, the continuing evolution of the mammal groups during the Tertiary Period with its beginning during the Paleocene sixty-five million years ago and ending with the Pliocene five-and-a-half million years ago, saw the appearance of the

beaver and the early beginnings of man. Some of the first
inhabitants of Wyoming butchered a mammoth southwest of
Brownsville over eleven thousand years ago.

South of Brownsville is Bridger's Pass, and Fort Bridger is
one hundred-fifty miles straight west. Bridger's Pass is just
thirty miles southwest of the Platte River rail crossing. The
Continental Divide, in its northwesterly course splits into an
eastern ridge of just under seven thousand feet and a western
rim of the same altitude. The divide meanders to enclose a
great basin almost circular in shape that is once more joined
in a singular spine seven miles southwest of South Pass.

The waters on the west side of the divide flow into the
Pacific and on the east into the Atlantic; however, the waters
inside this Great Divide Basin have no way out and flow into
the sand and disappear. In the process, the red rock and soil
is brought to the surface as the Red Desert. The rainfall here
is scanty; the winter, harsh; the summer heat, stifling; the
winds incredible and water lacking.

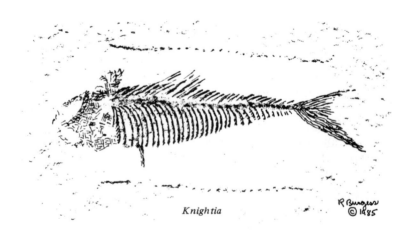

Knightia

CHAPTER THREE

MISS AMY STAFFORD

"Another busy night, Miss Stafford? You look lovely as always."

"Thank you, Edward," she told the dealer.

Twenty-dollar gold pieces changed hands rapidly on the noisy floor of the casino. Gleeful shouts came from the roulette table.

"Miss Stafford, Mr. Hilderbrandt wants five hundred."

"Of course," she said, initialing the note.

"Amy, darling, your gown is divine. Where did you get it? Paris?"

"Mrs. LaFleau, so good to see you. Henré is winning again, I see." She smiled politely.

"Miss Stafford, the gentleman wishes to play poker with you."

A handsome young lieutenant stood, patiently waiting, at a table.

"Tell him some other time, Freddie."

"Yes, Miss Stafford."

On a raised stage overlooking the lavish decor of the "Golden Belle" a string ensemble played Mozart.

Amy looked about the casino at the rich tapestries, fine European paintings and overcrowded gaming tables with satisfaction.

"Amy, dear, my offer still stands," said an immaculately dressed middle-aged man.

She had been offered a handsome price for her business on several occasions, but nothing to compare with this most generous proposal.

"I'll think about it, Mr. Carlisle."

"You have been saying that for weeks. I will pay you in gold. In full. Just name the date." He seemed agitated, scolding in manner, with a frown across his forehead and at the corners of his mouth. He was accustomed to getting his way. But so was Amy.

"I am not ready to sell. Not just yet." she smiled.

"A woman as young and beautiful as you should be traveling. Enjoying life. Seeing the world. Why, you have hardly been out of New Orleans."

"But I don't need those things. Just look around you. I have everything right here. And besides, I spent several years in Europe."

"Everything, my dear?"

"In gold, Mr. Carlisle?"

"In gold," he answered.

"Miss Stafford, the floor manager is ready."

"Thank you."

She turned to Mr. Carlisle, "Will you excuse me?"

"By all means," he said.

Amy walked the length of the floor to the casino's bank, and the armed guard admitted her.

"A very profitable night, Miss Stafford. Everything is in order."

The evening shift had changed, and it was time to check

out. On a long table in the middle of the room gold coins, arranged in five-hundred dollar stacks, glittered softly. Amy looked down the rows of gold and asked for the day book. She initialed the entry and handed it back.

"Splendid, Freddie."

Two armed guards wheeled the table into the vault and closed the heavy iron door.

"Will there be anything else, Miss Stafford?" asked a guard.

"No. That will be all, thank you."

"Goodnight, Miss Stafford," said a guard. "Your carriage is waiting."

"Goodnight, Phillip," she said.

A light rain was falling along the riverfront as the team of matched grays trotted briskly through the streets. She liked being alone at this time of night riding on the bricks where she had played as a child. In the golden lamp-light she saw the vacant lot, with the trees that had grown up, and where she received her first kiss. Funny, she thought, "I don't even remember his name."

Having been a strict disciplinarian, Amy's father had insisted that Amy obtain the best education possible. He was a graduate of Virginia Military Institute and had she been a boy, that fine institution would have been her alma mater. Instead, he had sent her to Paris for four years where she studied literature. Honoré De Balzac's *Pere Goriot* was one of her favorite works, for she saw a little of Eugene de Rastignac in herself. Rastignac had been in Paris to study law while his family struggled to send him twelve-hundred francs a year. Assuredly, there was a lot of Father Goriot in her own personality: money, ambition, a search for identity, a search for the absolute. As she had followed Dostoevsky's interest in Balzac's *Eugenie Grandet*, she developed an intense interest in Fyodor Dostoevsky's writings. Much like her father, Dostoevsky had studied in a military engineering school. She shared Dostoevsky's passion for Shakespeare, Goethe, Homer, Hugo, Pushkin and Gogol.

The wheels of the carriage splashed water against the sides and undercarriage of the coach, almost obliterating the sounds of the horse's shod feet on the bricks. She thought of her father's long explanation of the purchase of Louisiana Territory and his interest in the country west of the Mississippi.

"If I were a young man," he had said, "I would make my way to the mountains. Maybe on to the Pacific Ocean. To California, or to Oregon. There's a future out there, Amy. I've known it all along. Just as President Thomas Jefferson must have known it after he had read of Alexander Mackenzie's attempt to find the Northwest Passage in 1789. It seems the British and French were uninterested in Mackenzie's report even after he reached the Pacific by following the Peace River to the ocean. 'Couldn't get ships across Canada,' they snorted. But Old Tom Jefferson paid attention to Mackenzie. He read his book. And after Napoleon lost two armies in Santo Domingo in 1802, France was short of money, so who do you think was standing in the wings with a sack full of coin? That's right. President Jefferson. Bought the Louisiana Territory in 1803. Biggest damn steal in history!"

Major Stafford had slapped his knee and laughed. "Jefferson already had it planned. He sent Meriweather Lewis and William Clark up the Missouri. Manuel Lisa supplied them in St. Louis. John Colter was a member of that Lewis and Clark party, and after they reached the Pacific Ocean by going down the Columbia River, they returned to St. Louis in 1806. If I remember correctly, John Colter stayed in the mountains for four more years, and then Manuel Lisa had his own party of Kentucky trappers ready to follow Lewis and Clark's trail up the Missouri. During 1807 several trappers including Andrew Henry, John Hoback, Edward Robinson and Jacob Reznor had headed up river with Lisa. Colter had fallen in with them and showed Lisa a good site for a fort at the junction of the Bighorn where it empties into the Yellowstone." Bruce Stafford settled back in his chair, his face flushed. The Major got excited when he talked to Amy about the west.

"As much as you like all this history, father, it surprises me that you weren't a mountain man." she had said.

"I could see the Civil War coming on or I would have been." he had exclaimed. "Of course, the beaver were no longer valuable by the time I was a young man. In the early '40's the silk hat had finished the demand for beaver in Europe. But let me finish my story. Old John Jacob Astor had already made his fortune trading with China by shipping eastern furs around the Horn in his own fleet of ships, but he wanted the western fur trade too, so he sent Wilson Price Hunt from St. Louis up the Missouri. And to make sure he got a party through, old Astor sent the ship *Tonquin* around the Horn to the mouth of the Columbia. The *Tonquin* met with disaster during a stormy beaching at the mouth of the Columbia and was later burned by Indians. Meanwhile, Hunt's party had run across John Colter on the Missouri River. That old Colter seemed to be everywhere. Well, Colter told Hunt to avoid the river route since the Blackfeet were very unfriendly!" Again, he slapped his knee. "Stripped Colter of his clothes in 1808 somewhere around the head-waters of the Yellowstone River and chased him one hundred sixty-five miles back to Fort Manuel. That's how unfriendly they were."

"Well, old Colter had shown Hunt how to get over the mountains through a pass south of the Missouri at the head of Wind River. Union Pass it's called. Hunt confirmed Colter's story after he talked later with John Hoback who had trapped on south of Union Pass in 1810 on the Hoback River. Hunt had lost about a third of his party when they tried to float down the Snake River into the Columbia. They weren't much luckier after arriving at the mouth of the Columbia on the Pacific Ocean because the War of 1812 had forced the sale of their post to the British Northwest Company. That's when Robert Stuart led a party of seven back through South Pass and down the Sweetwater in 1812. They wintered at Red Buttes on the Platte just west of where Fort Caspar later got located."

"But, father," Amy had said, "it's a land of sand and savages. Why on earth would anyone want to go there?"

"It was Zebulon Pike in 1806 who first started the 'Great American Desert' story. He didn't get up into the Sweetwater Country. Major Andrew Henry had trapped with Manuel Lisa on the headwaters of the Yellowstone during 1811, but it got too tough and they pulled back to St. Louis. Major Stephen Long, in 1820 led an expedition up the Platte and South Platte looking for the Red River. Didn't find it. When he returned, he said that that country was 'almost wholly unfit for cultivation.' I was too young for the Ashley-Henry hunting party up the Missouri in 1822 and 1823, but by God, I would have loved that trip!"

She had smiled at her father, and did not speak.

"Don't you see, Amy? The key to the settlement of the West is on the Sweetwater."

The carriage had passed the bordello district and several noisy saloons when she tapped on the carriage window where the driver rode.

"Yes, Miss Stafford," she heard him say, as the horses slowed and stopped.

"I'll only be thirty minutes," she told the driver.

"Yes, Madame."

She entered the Lamplighter Cabaret where the maitre d' greeted her, "Miss Stafford. So good to see you. Your table is waiting." He ushered her through the crowded room to a table near the entertainment stage.

"Your usual, Miss Amy?"

"Yes, please."

She loved to relax before retiring for the night. After a busy day handling all that money, it was refreshing to forget about gold. She looked about the room and saw familiar faces who nodded greetings to her.

"May I join you, Miss Stafford?"

"No," she replied simply.

"May I see you home after the show?"

"No, Harold, I don't think your wife would approve," she said coldly.

She noticed glances toward her table from many women in the room. She finished her drink and got up to leave.

"So soon, Miss Stafford?" asked her waiter. "Is everything all right?"

"Yes, everything is just fine," she said.

Outside, the rain had increased and was coming down in heavy sheets. Even though there was a canopy entryway, the rain sent a shiver through her as she stepped into the carriage. She was upset, angry and restless as the coach moved quickly through the rain and finally turned up the tree bordered lane to the front entrance to her home. She dashed the few feet through the rain and the butler let her in.

"Nasty tonight, Miss Amy. And cold. I don't like the cold."

"I will be sleeping late in the morning, Samuel. I will have breakfast at ten."

"I have a fire in your room, Miss Amy. May I bring you a cup of hot tea? You'll catch your death of pneumonia. Your father would have a fit if he saw you wet like this. I'll swear, child, you're going to have to start taking better care of yourself."

"Thank you, Samuel, but I think I will go right to bed."

"Goodnight," he said.

"Goodnight," she replied as she climbed the stairway to her bedroom. A warm fire burned in the fireplace, but she still felt the cold.

She dried her long, black, rainsoaked hair with a towel and brushed it. Quickly changing into her nightgown she turned back the covers and slipped into bed pulling her pillow tightly to her.

"I'm cold," she thought, as she drifted off to sleep.

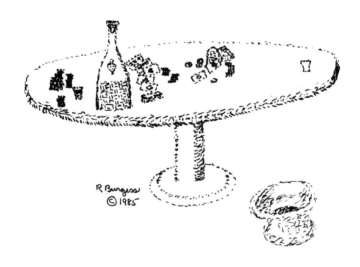

R Burgess
© 1985

CHAPTER FOUR

JULY 1868

The packhorse picked his way down the long, steep canyon. The day's last rays of light made the tangle of fallen trees difficult to avoid. The man heard, mingled with the sounds of small rocks kicked down the hill by the fast walking pair of horses, a sharp, scraping noise of branches springing off the canvas pack cover.

Jedediah Caldwell was in a hurry. He wanted to strike the headwaters of the Platte River before he stopped for the day. He was two days out of Denver and his horses were tiring.

Twenty-five years earlier John Fremont had used this game trail up the Cache La Poudre River to enter the Laramie Plains across Wagonhound Creek. After skirting Elk Mountain in Dakota Territory, he had crossed the Platte at about the same spot that Jedediah expected to be after his third long day's ride. Across this deep, slow moving river a railroad bridge was being built in a race to cross the Red Desert.

The rider saw the river below him and picked up his pace.

A thick clump of pine trees with an outcropping of rock would make a good camp.

"Hell, horse," he muttered aloud, as he untied the diamond on the pack, "only one more day of this gutbuster, and we'll be there." He set the heavy canvas packsaddles on the ground on each side of the horse, uncinched the sawbuck and threw it on a fallen tree-trunk. He now turned to his mount and unsaddled him. From the packsack he found his light canvas nosebags which he filled with grain for the horses' rations. A thick bed of pine needles under the ledge of rock served as a mattress for his bedroll.

He broke some twigs from the lower dead branches of a tree and lit his fire. Into the heavy black skillet he cut thick slices of bacon off a large slab. The handle was still cold as he set the skillet to the back of the fire. "I sure like this old coffee pot," he thought, as he dipped it full of water from the Platte. Its blackened sides, from many campfires, lent character to its many dents and chips. He untied the rawhide string around the sack of coffee and poured a thick layer of grounds on top of the cold water. Three tin pans served for cooking, eating and mixing and into one he put a handful of flour and then added a glob of bacon grease and squeezed it in with his hands, while adding a pinch of salt and a little baking powder. He slowly added water to make a stiff dough and then pinched off a chunk, working it into a thin patty with his hands. He removed the bacon from the hot skillet, leaving a little grease in the bottom and tossed in the bannock. "Griddlecakes, fried bread or bannock, it's good whatever you call it," he thought, "Howie will have buffalo steaks for us tomorrow night."

He had been in Denver washing the sand out of his beard when he received the telegraph message:

JED. BRING GEAR. STOP MEET ME RAIL
CROSSING PLATTE. STOP GOLD STOLEN.
STOP HOWIE.

"Two hundred miles in three days," he thought, "Hell, not bad for a thirty-five year old mountain man. When I was twenty, I would have done it in two."

He had ridden through a rain storm during the early afternoon and his weapons would need cleaning. In his saddle scabbard, which he carried under his left leg with the butt to the rear, was a .44 Henry rimfire 16 shot lever action rifle. Its cartridge fired a 216 grain bullet with a 25 grain blackpowder charge. It would penetrate 8 inches of pine at 100 yards. Jedediah picked out a piece of crisp bacon from his plate and stuck it in his mouth while walking back to his saddle. A double barreled .12 bore percussion shotgun was stuck through a leather sling on the saddle horn. A 60 grain blackpowder charge propelled an ounce and a quarter of buckshot with deadly efficiency. He had cut the barrels to 15 inches to make it handle better from horseback. A powder flask and pouch for his buckshot was in his saddle bags. He poured a steaming cup of coffee and drank.

His sidearm was a Remington .44 Army percussion revolver. Its 8 inch octagon barrel was blued; its hammer case-hardened. He carried the second of a matched pair in his saddle bags. Skin cartridges made by Hazard Powder Company and packed six to the box were also in his saddle bags. Percussion caps were in a small tin box. He had learned to repair his guns and carried a small bag of spare parts and tools including screw drivers, stones, hones, small files, drift punches, main springs, screws, hands, sears, and sights. He disassembled the .44 and carefully oiled each part and then reassembled the pistol and wiped off the excess oil. "A man without guns in this wilderness is a man in trouble," he knew.

Nine years before he had seen piles of bodies of men who had starved to death after leaving Denver when the Cherry Creek gold strike had fizzled. They had been ill-prepared and poorly accoutered. Each and every one had expected to strike it rich. They had come from all the professions and were a cross section of men on the frontier. Many of them had walked to Colorado and hadn't even brought a gold pan. They believed that the pickens were easy, and minor details like supplies and shelter, the quibbling of skeptics.

Now his horses threw their heads up to get the last morsels of grain and pawed at the ground for more. He hobbled one forefoot of each horse and tied a twenty-five foot rawhide lariat to the iron ring of each hobble. He then drove a picket pin deep into the ground and threw a half hitch over it. The grass along the banks of the Platte was deep. These horses would have full bellies come morning. But; to the north, in the Red Desert, the grass was scanty, short and scarce.

While he was sure that Howie would have a pack string of mules loaded with supplies, Jed knew the importance of an abundance of ammunition. He had purchased one thousand rounds of .44 Henry, two hundred rounds of .44 revolver and ten pounds of buckshot. The ammunition weighed about fifty pounds. In addition, he had five pounds of blackpowder and a sack of wads for the shotgun.

A three-piece ramrod with a slotted tip he used to oil each firearm. For his shotgun, he first pulled the overshot wad and dumped out the buckshot and then pulled the overpowder wad and dumped the powder, which was damp. He ran an oily rag down the bore and dried it with a clean patch. He charged each barrel with sixty grains of blackpowder, firmly seated an overpowder wad, poured in an ounce and a quarter of buckshot, rammed home an overshot wad and recapped the nipples with fresh primers. He laid the shotgun on his bed and oiled the other weapons.

At the head of his bedroll he placed his saddle and along side he arranged his panniers, which were canvas packsacks whose corners were reenforced with leather strips that were riveted into place, and hand sewn with heavy waxed thread. They measured about twenty-two inches wide, twenty inches tall and twelve inches deep. With two leather loops attached to the back of each pannier they were easily hung from the oak crossbucks of the packsaddle. In the southwest they were called aparejos. He unrolled his blankets and threw the canvas pack cover over the whole affair.

He had come a long distance up a steep canyon whose swift river had carved deep gorges and wide meadows through rugged rocks of brown, black, gray and gold.

"I wonder what Howie has got himself into?" he thought. "We had some great times together along the Bozeman Trail. He's turned into a regular solid citizen. Next thing he'll have him a wife and a house back in Omaha."

He reached over and poured himself the last of the coffee and picked out the remaining bacon as twilight turned to darkness and his little camp closed around him.

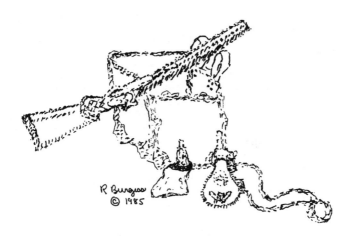

CHAPTER FIVE

THE SCOUT

Brown's Hotel at Fort Laramie in 1868 wasn't much of a place. Its low pitched roof with a sod cover complimented the low rolling country at the confluence of the Laramie and Platte Rivers. The axe hewn logs, slapped with mud to keep out the insistent Wyoming winds, made it a snug accommodation. Several log rooms, added as if as an afterthought, joined the main structure in mutual sympathy. Founded in 1834 as a fur trading post, this fort then called Fort William stood as a beacon for trappers and mountain men even after it became an army post in 1849.

Jimmy Lee Robineaux was rolling his "possibles" in a woolen blanket. Some men weren't comfortable in the wilds with a wagon load of goods, but even a frontiersman like Jimmy carried a few things with him that made survival likely and comfort possible. The mountain man and backwoodsman always carried these "possibles" which included flint and steel, a small sharp knife, an awl, needle and thread for both clothing repair and closing skin wounds, fishhooks and line, a sack of jerky and a parfleche of corn. His Shoshoni wife handed him a leather sack full of pemmican.

"You take good care of yourself, Jim," she said.

"I'll be back in two weeks, woman."

"You taking a pack horse?"

"No. I'll be at the Platte in two days. Howie will have extra horses and mules."

Jimmy's father had joined the Ashley-Henry hunting and trapping expedition in 1822 after reading a St. Louis newspaper announcement addressed "To Enterprising Young Men." It stated: "The subscriber wishes to engage one-hundred young men to ascend the Missouri River to its source, there to be employed one, two, or three years. For particulars inquire of Major Andrew Henry, near the lead mines, in the county of Washington, who will ascend with and command the party; or the subscriber, near St. Louis." It was signed — William H. Ashley.

Jimmy had been born near Three Forks on the Missouri in 1825. His father had been killed by Blackfeet at the headwaters of the Snake in 1841 when Jimmy was 16 years old. French and woodcraft were the legacies of childhood; marksmanship and trapping were the teachings of boyhood; horsemanship and Indian ways were the daily instructions under the watchful eyes of his father. It was natural that he should take a Shoshoni squaw as a wife for there were few white women on this frontier, and besides, his mother had been Indian.

Shoshoni language and customs were the birthright from his mother. Discipline and honor were her teachings in his childhood. Obedience and duty were her examples which he learned during long winter days in a tepee. Some of his fondest memories, which he still recalled often, were long summer afternoons spent watching his mother fashion soft leather skins into beautiful leggins, moccasins, shirts and breeches. She had died during the fall of 1834.

Jimmy had worked as a guide for the army until two years ago, and for the past eighteen months he had escorted wagon trains over the Oregon Trail as far as the Columbia River.

He knew the varieties of frontier's inhabitants, had met many whom he admired and reveled in the heroic tales of adventure. The folklore of the mountain man had begun when John Colter, a member of the Lewis and Clark Expedition of 1804 which ascended the Missouri, travelled to the mouth of the Columbia at the Pacific Ocean and returned to the Yellowstone country in 1806. Colter had been captured by Indians, stripped of his clothing and given a headstart in a footrace for his life, which he won. Another momentous trip, organized in St. Louis, led by Andrew Henry and participated in by men like Hugh Glass, James Clyman, Bill Sublette, Tom Fitzpatrick, Jedediah Smith, Jim Bridger, or "Old Gabe" as he was known throughout the West, and riverboat men like Jimmy's father produced the leavening for hundreds of stories told around campfires throughout the Rocky Mountain West.

Old Gabe was heading down river this year of 1868 and younger men like Jimmy Lee were scouts for expeditions of all kinds. When Howie was a cavalry officer, Jimmy had been one of his scouts along the Bozeman Trail. Jimmy liked the 39 year old Howard Prescott who was born in 1829 in Indiana, had joined the Union Army in 1860 and rapidly rose to the rank of Major by the war's end in 1865. He was assigned to New Orleans to enforce order after the war but was transferred to the West to command a company of cavalry at Fort Reno in 1866. With the rapid coming of the railroad in 1867, Howie, after resigning from the army in 1866, organized a lucrative enterprise developing his own freight and stage business carrying goods from End of Track to outlying settlers and miners. Now Howie had another job for Jimmy.

"Gold shipment stolen," Jimmy told his wife; "that should be the fixens for adventure."

"You watch your hair!" his wife exclaimed.

"That Injun ain't been born yet!" grinned Jimmy as he hugged her in his big arms.

He stood five feet ten inches in his moccasins and weighed one hundred eighty pounds. Dark black hair, cut to the collar, framed a short black moustache, the only hair on his clean shaven face. His sun-darkened, ruddy complexion told of a lifetime spent out-of-doors.

He wore a three-quarter length Hudson Bay blanket coat, made from a white blanket with red, black and yellow stripes and a shirt of gray flannel with small leather buttons. Buckskin trousers, held up with a wide leather belt and buckle given him by the harness maker at the fort, tapered into deerskin leggings with intricate beadwork ties sewn by his wife. On his feet, elk skin moccasins with hard moose hide innersoles gave some comfort to long hours in the saddle. A red woolen cap, its tall soft crown drooped to the left, completed his dress.

Jimmy walked to the bed, picked up a heavy leather belt, threaded a long leather knife sheath on it and buckled it around his waist. This famous Green River butcher knife thrust into the case did not take its name from the river of mountain man fame in the West, but rather from the Green River in Massachusetts on whose banks John Russell had built a factory with stamping machines where he shaped and forged his famous blades stamped "J. Russell and Co. Green River Works." Many a varmint, socked, "Clean up to Green River," never lived to tell about it.

Hatchet, tomahawk, belt axe and Yankee axe with short handle were all names of the same tool found useful to both mountain man and Indian. Jimmy's belt axe, marked "U.S." on the blade, balanced nicely and rode comfortably at the small of his back, its fourteen-inch handle stuck through his belt.

He chose his best horse, a big tough bay gelding, nine years old and dependable. Strong and with a big heart, the horse liked to run and loved the chase. His saddle, a Mexican rig, had a boot on the left side of the horn through which he stuck his Spencer .52 caliber rimfire repeater. Its magazine held seven rounds. Tied right beside it was a Blakeslee cartridge box, cavalry size, which contained ten tubes, each with 7 cartridges. On the right side of the horn was a heavy leather holster holding his Walker Colt Dragoon .44 revolver. It weighed four pounds, but hell, the horse was going to carry it! He had cut the 7½ inch barrel of his Colt 1860 Army .44 to 2½ inches for use as a hideout gun. This he carried in his saddle bag.

In a saddle boot under his leg on the left side was his buffalo rifle. This Sharps, .52 caliber, slant breech, percussion, 1852 patent, with a 27-inch browned barrel of #3 weight had double-set triggers. He carried linen cartridges and used musket caps on the nipple.

A rawhide lariat, used mostly to graze his horse, and a flannel covered canteen completed his saddle. He tied his blanket roll of "possibles" behind the cantle adding a sack of grain for two days' rations for his horse and swung himself into the saddle.

"Two weeks," he said to his squaw as he started up the Laramie River.

A small band of Arapaho, camped one mile outside the fort on the river, silently watched him ride right through it. They were mostly women and children.

Congress had sent out the Peace Commission a year and a half before in an effort to stop the Sioux War. The Sioux had agreed to a reservation in Dakota Territory in 1866, and several of the Plains Tribes accepted reservations in Oklahoma.

The younger bucks were getting restless, including the Arapaho, Cheyenne and Sioux. On the Southern Plains the Comanche, Kiowa and Apache were raiding emigrant trains, miners and settlers.

Now the railroad was to change forever the Indian influence in the West. One year before, in 1867, the town of Cheyenne, known as "End of Track" by the rail-laying crew, saw Fort Russell established on Crow Creek where there were eleven hundred troops garrisoned. Already, thousands of people were riding in passenger cars while thousands of tons of freight were being handled economically over the rails. Railroads had been first established west of the Mississippi in 1852 following decades of debate in Congress for a transcontinental system. Daniel Webster argued the absurdity of developing this wasteland "of deserts, of shifting sands and whirlwinds of dust, of cactus and prairie dogs." Just as the Butterfield Overland stage route through the south lost out with the Civil War of the sixties, so had the southern transcontinental rail route through Texas and New Mexico. In the meantime Theodore Judah and Grenville Dodge, surveyors, had completed routes through the center of the developing new nation while Jefferson Davis' southern proposal derailed.

Red Cloud. Crazy Horse. Those Sioux leaders, wary of the white man's intrusion into their hunting grounds following the Gold Rush to California in 1849, reluctantly watched as tens of thousands of gold seekers traveled up the Platte and through South Pass in the spring of 1851. Tom Fitzpatrick, one of the first white men through South Pass, watched those thousands of emigrants from his base of operations where he was the Indian Agent at Fort Laramie. Hunger and disease, especially cholera, had followed the emigrants and affected the Indians, and Fitzpatrick had heard complaints from both sides. Evolving from those disputes and with the sanction of Congress, Fitzpatrick skillfully assembled members of most of the aggrieved tribes. Even the Crows had been represented in spite of the attendance of their ancient enemy, the Sioux; and both those tribes, who heretofore had not accepted boundaries, now agreed to territorial definitions and in turn were reassured payment from the government.

That understanding had failed after only three years when in 1854, the Indians, assembled outside the walls of Fort Laramie to receive payment for their part of the treaty, became embroiled in an incident involving a Sioux brave who had shot a cow and fled to the Indian camp for protection. The arresting officer, Lt. John Grattan, tried unsuccessfully to persuade the Sioux leaders to release the brave. When they refused, he ordered his troopers to open fire, and in the battle that followed, he and his entire party were destroyed. The experiment between Plains Indians and government negotiators had died with them.

To the south, William Bent, the Indian Agent had established his fort on the Arkansas River, married a Cheyenne woman, spoke their language and did well until the Colorado Gold Rush of 1858 and 1859 brought in hordes of miners with the inevitable conflict between Indian and white. Bent, who had befriended the Indians, thought it in their best interest to cooperate with the government whereupon he had persuaded the Southern Plains Indians to agree to a treaty reducing their territory. Two years later in 1861 and 1862 the Navaho and Apache even farther south had started their raids on settlements which prompted Kit Carson, with his Volunteers, to move out of New Mexico to start a military campaign against them. After little more than a year of Carson's destruction of their wheat and cornfields, the Navaho surrendered while the Apache continued to raid. In the North, Red Cloud observed but did not smile.

By contrast the Santee Sioux in Minnesota in 1862 had reacted with violent fury in response to broken treaty guarantees which assured them almost two million dollars in payment for over twenty million acres of property. Over four hundred whites had been killed when the army and civilians in Minnesota under Colonel Henry Sibley took four weeks to defeat the Sioux. Then farther south, in Colorado, along Sand Creek in 1864, Black Kettle had established his winter camp of almost five hundred Cheyenne, mostly women and children, with the belief that his long efforts of peace with the white man were coming to fruition. A former Methodist minister, Colonel J.M. Chivington, the commander of the Military District of Colorado, had other than peaceful intentions in mind when emotions were at a fever pitch following atrocities against emigrant trains and settlers east of Denver. After death the bodies of emigrants and miners were mutilated in the belief that the spirit of the slain would be similarly disfigured in the afterlife.

Warm buffalo robes were little comfort to Chief Black Kettle and Chief White Antelope as their Cheyenne village awakened to rifle and cannon fire. Almost one hundred women and children were killed as well as Chief White Antelope whose scrotum was cut off to be used as a tobacco pouch by a soldier. However, Black Kettle escaped with his wounded wife. The Plains Indian, especially the Cheyenne, Arapaho and Sioux now became infuriated. The government responded with a crusade to civilize the Indian. The official policy stated: "Feed him; clothe him; teach him religious doctrine; appoint Indian agents sympathetic to religious teachings; and above all, let him continue to hunt buffalo."

With the discovery of gold and silver in Virginia City, Montana, freighters supplied the camps from riverboats steaming up the Missouri from St. Louis. In 1852 a French half-breed discovered gold in Montana, but gold fields were not developed until a group of unsuccessful returning California miners, five years later in 1857 turned north off the Oregon Trail to follow up reports of gold in the mountain valleys somewhere near the headwaters of the Missouri. In 1861 gold was found in paying quantities, and in 1862 the

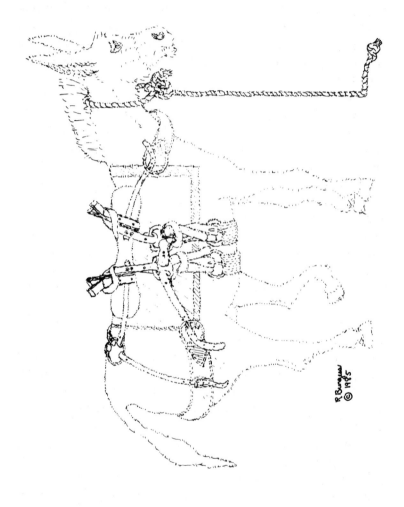

Alder Gulch sands yielded fabulous amounts of gold dust. Thousands of adventurers swarmed into the several mile long valley, and by the end of the first year millions of dollars in dust and nuggets were in the pokes of hard working miners. They built Virginia City, Montana, in Alder Gulch and like the "End of Track" tent cities and mining towns throughout the West, attracted every type of undesirable looking for a quick buck and easy fortune.

By then the Bozeman Trail had become a major source of supply as it branched north off the Oregon Trail above Fort Laramie. The Bozeman Trail, after crossing the Powder River, Crazy Woman Creek, and the Bighorn River north of the Bighorn Mountains had deteriorated dangerously and turned into a route whose travelers were fodder for hostile Sioux. Meanwhile, in 1864 Jim Bridger had led an emigrant group of miners to the gold fields of Virginia City, Montana. There were sixty-two wagons and over three hundred people traveling by a route south of the Bighorn Mountains. Bridger hoped to avoid the Sioux by following the Platte to Red Buttes, and then north to the Bighorn River. He only encountered friendly Shoshone Indians on that trip.

Red Cloud had watched those freight wagons and still did not smile. His attacks on those invaders had culminated in a meeting of Indians and whites at Fort Laramie in 1866. Red Cloud, Spotted Tail, Man Afraid of His Horses and others were astonished as Colonel Henry Carrington told of his orders to establish forts along the Bozeman Trail. Red Cloud left the meeting in obvious anger, although remaining chiefs continued to negotiate and finally signed a treaty allowing Forts Phil Kearny, Reno and C.F. Smith to be garrisoned and in exchange accepted promises that all lands north of the Platte were to be forever Indian lands. Then by 1866, as soon as those forts were established, Red Cloud began his attacks. Supply wagon trains, wood details, and work parties were under constant fire. Progress for building a transcontinental railroad was seriously hampered by Red Cloud's agressive warfare. By now only war became the way to settle what negotiation did not.

Then William J. Fetterman made his fatal decision. A captain under Carrington's command at Fort Phil Kearny, Fetterman and a troop of eighty cavalry rode out of the fort to rescue a wood gathering detail under attack and were drawn into an ambush by a warrior of Red Cloud's named Crazy Horse. Even though explicit instructions from Carrington to Fetterman not to pursue beyond Lodge Trail Ridge had been issued, Fetterman ordered his troop forward. An overwhelming force of Indians who had assembled out of sight in the surrounding hills rained arrows on the party as men and animals alike died. By the end of the day not a trooper lived. Red Cloud's grim resolve was to drive the white man from Indian lands.

All of those were the often-told events of the Indian lands. Indian lands, now travelled by Jimmy Lee Robineaux through the Laramie Mountains. "Laramie River, Laramie City, Fort Laramie, Laramie Peak, Laramie Mountains, Laramie Plains," he thought; "that Jacques LaRamie must have been quite a man. I'll bet my dad knew him. I never heard him talk about him, however. Old Bridger never mentioned him either. That Jacques sure did get around."

The emigrants on the Oregon Trail had been favorite Indian targets before the railroad construction crews moved along the newly laid track. Now the Sioux attacked grading parties far ahead of End of Track, and they had been raiding since the eastern plains of Dakota Territory had been entered. Then when gold was discovered at South Pass City in 1867 the freight lines and mining camps with their horses, mules and supplies were all vulnerable. The Bozeman Trail, used heavily to freight supplies to Virginia City, Montana miners and several forts, enjoyed less and less traffic these days because the Sioux controlled the lands north of the Platte. Just eighteen months before in December, 1866 the Fetterman massacre had occurred.

When the summer rendezvous was in its heyday during 1837 and before its wane three years later William Drummond Stewart headed for the Green River for adventure and big game hunting. He took Alfred Jacob Miller with him to record his escapades on canvas.

Later in 1843 when the Oregon Trail was just earning its name, Stewart outfitted again for a sporting trip West. He took a wagon, ten carts, and fifty of the best horses obtainable and proceeded to slaughter buffalo for sport, eating just the hump and tongue. He spent two weeks on Fremont Lake in the Wind River Mountains using a fifteen-man India-rubber boat carried by wagon along with tinned meats, fine wines, a barrel of alcohol and other luxurious trappings.

"There wasn't much interest in this part of the country during the Civil War, but it's sure hopping now," he mused. "That damn railroad has split the buffalo herd in two. Now the 'sports' are shooting from the railroad passenger cars just to see them fall. Won't be many left in another ten years."

Later that afternoon, topping out on Laramie Mountain, he headed north for a few miles to pick up the Medicine Bow River. Jimmy sighted an Arapaho brave at the bottom of a grassy, sage brush-covered hill; the Indian, sitting on his war pony, held a lance and a tomahawk. His face, painted for battle, appeared expressionless.

"Well, old hoss," Jimmy mumbled to himself, "plenty of singing and dancing in camp tonight if this young buck can pull this off."

Jimmy offered peace but knew it was futile. He advanced at a trot. The Indian brave lowered his lance and approached at a gallop. Then when there were only fifteen yards between them, Jimmy swung under the neck of his bay and turned him sharply to the left. The two horses crashed together with a loud thud. Both riders fell to the ground, rolled to their feet and circled, looking for an opening. The Indian, now armed with a tomahawk, cautiously waited. Jimmy drew his knife and in a fierce struggle, buried it under the ribs of the warrior. On the ridge to the north a small war party had watched the whole quick episode; they then turned, held an animated conference and with a flourish, brandished weapons above their heads in an ostentatious display of anger. Eagerly, amid shouts, they bounded down the ridge toward the big bay and its rider.

The bay sensed the excitement and needed no urging by its master. In a long, smooth lope the grain-fed horse easily outdistenced the smaller Indian horses. Far to the rear Jimmy saw the last Indian brave stop, turn and give up the chase.

There would be good grass on the head of the Medicine Bow. Even now he could see small herds of buffalo in all directions. The white rumps of antelope stood out plainly in the browning late summer grass.

"I will ride until dark" he thought. No fire tonight on these open plains. Laramie Peak stood night watch to the north. The changing light of sunset, which never ceased to fascinate him, ushered in the night noises of the plains. The coyotes plaintive howl reminded him of the September elk bugle. It was already getting cold at night and it was just the first week of July. "I haven't laid in my winter meat supply," he thought, "I'll have to get busy when I get back."

In 1857 the first workable pair of field glasses had been perfected, further development and production during the Civil War making the glasses readily available to frontiersmen like Jimmy. With his field glasses he searched down the tributary of the Medicine Bow River and then around the horizon; finally satisfied that all was quiet, he stopped for the night. A front foot picket secured his horse. He fed half the grain to the bay and saved the rest for morning. For his own supper he unwrapped a dark cake of pemmican which his wife had prepared from equal parts of pounded buffalo jerky and rendered fat. She had mixed in dried currant berries gathered from thick patches along the Laramie River. Shelled corn, first steamed in a skillet and then lightly fried in bacon grease, salted and carried in a small sack made the perfect traveling ration. "Damn, I wish I had a cup of coffee," he thought, "but I don't dare strike a fire. No moon tonight. Most varmints will sit tight until dawn. I wonder who Howie has gathered for this party?"

CHAPTER SIX

LARAMIE CITY

A long, wailing steam whistle broke the silence of the four gamblers sitting at the elegant table in the gently swaying private coach of the railroad car. Gambling was a welcome diversion from the boring trip across the monotonous prairie grasslands of Nebraska. Overstuffed chairs with walnut end tables supported silver trays with decanters full of brandies and wines. Hundreds of gamblers plied their trade along this route.

The rhythmical clacking of the wheels striking each joint in the hastily laid track was the only sound that could be heard at the table of the nattily dressed men.

"We're slowing down," said a small weasel-faced gambler.

Charles Richfield stuck his head out the window and said, "Buffalo."

Some of the smaller herds would hardly slow the train from its average of fifteen miles per hour, but this herd was a big one. Out in the Powder River country Charles had seen herds of thousands of buffalo when he was stationed at Fort Phil Kearny two years ago.

Earlier Richfield had first met Howard Prescott while serving under his command in a cavalry company along the Bozeman Trail. He had found Howie an efficient, fair, disciplined leader of men. He wasn't surprised later when he learned that Howie had started his own stage and freight line after he was mustered out of the army in 1866. What had begun as two wagons and eight mules had grown into dozens of wagons and stages and at least five hundred horses and mules. Howie had been freighting from End of Track and supplying mining camps in the Sweetwater country. Obviously he had done well with the enterprise.

"Sounds like he's got trouble now," he thought.

In Omaha the telegraph message to Charles had stated:

COME TO END OF TRACK. STOP FREIGHT LINE HELD UP. STOP GOLD TAKEN. STOP HOWIE

"Your bet, Slick," said the weasel.

"I'll open for a hundred," said Chuck.

"I'd get my mind on the game," said Jack, "or I'd go watch the buffalo!"

"Don't be a sore loser, Jack," said the weasel.

Jack had lost five hundred dollars, and he wasn't taking it kindly, "Go to hell!" he snarled; "I've had about enough of your smirking. I'll cut your ears off!" he added as he pulled a long Arkansas toothpick from his boot.

"Back off, friend," Richfield stated calmly.

"Friend, hell! You want a piece of this, do you, Slick?" stated Jack, waving the knife.

At this challenge Charles drew his Navy Colt from his shoulder holster and struck Jack across the face, setting his nose over under his eye and sending him crashing to the floor.

"Get up and I'll kill you!" Charles said.

Jack lay there with a whimper and didn't move.

"Think I'll go watch the buffalo," Charles said as he picked up his gold coins; "the company will be better in another car."

Charles Richfield liked fine clothes, well-made boots, tastefully engraved firearms, Kentucky whiskey, poker, adventure and women. He had brought an ornately carved wooden trunk in the baggage car which contained the accoutrements needed for his desert journey.

This train, ten cars long, had traveled for two days without interruption after leaving Omaha. Now it had stopped and was delayed five hours while waiting for the herd of buffalo to pass.

Charles walked through the passenger car full of gamblers, prospectors, miners, prostitutes, muleskinners, hustlers, pimps, and railroad construction workers of all kinds. Wherever he looked, he could see Faro and games of three card monte in progress throughout the coach but very little interest in the buffalo herd. One older woman, a Faro dealer, was teaching a young new recruit the ways of survival. The youngster wasn't making any money on this run, but the pretty young girl would turn to a more lucrative profession when they reached End of Track. There was money to be made from the thousands of men working on the crossing of the continent. There were surveyors and graders, freighters, laborers, and now camp followers. Saloon keepers could acquire collapsible canvas and board tents complete with imitation wood with false fronts in Chicago for three hundred dollars. It took two to three hours to assemble these places of business once they arrived at the Platte River.

Richfield walked into a half-empty passenger car and saw, sitting alone, and half asleep a stern looking, black bearded, robust man with dark eyes who seemed to be frowning at the buffalo. Charles addressed him, "Mind if I join you?"

The man looked up, didn't answer, but nodded his approval.

Charles sat down, stretched his legs and offered, "Going far?"

"End of Track."

"Have you been there before?"

The bearded man opened his mouth slightly, licked his lips, but didn't speak. After a long pause he changed his mind and said, "Yes, sir. I've been there. May name is Jack Casement. I'm the track laying contractor for the Union Pacific Railroad. Are you looking for a job?"

"No, I've got a job, Mr. Casement. My name is Charles Richfield. I received a wire from my good friend Howard Prescott. I'm going to End of Track to help him in any way I can."

"Major Prescott's in trouble is he? Well, it doesn't surprise me. The damn Sioux have been giving us fits!"

"I'm not sure it's the Sioux, General."

Jack Casement looked at Charles through narrowed eyes. "Army man are you?"

"Yes, sir. I was Major Prescott's first sergeant on the Powder River."

"How long since you soldiered last?"

"A year and a half ago. March, 1867. Three months after the Fetterman Massacre."

"If Fetterman had listened to orders, it wouldn't have happened," thought Richfield.

"Major Prescott led our company out of Fort Reno on the Powder up to Fort Phil Kearny. We arrived two days after they buried the dead. It was a dismal sight. Eighty troopers killed. It reminded me of Vicksburg, only smaller."

"It's a violent world, sergeant."

"Yes, sir." He paused, set his jaw and added, "And crooked."

Casement raised his eyebrows, but didn't respond.

"Now you take this railroad," began Charles Richfield; "talk has it that the Credit Mobilier is a swindle and that

some fella named George Francis Train brought the idea
from France as a way to finance the building of this transcontinental line. Seems the stockholders of the Credit Mobilier
are also the owners and directors of the Union Pacific."

"Where did you hear that?" asked Casement. An embarrassed red flush crossed his face.

"Omaha. Everybody's talking about it; Rumors. Whispering
about Doctor Durant, Oakes and Oliver Ames; Gossip. Lots
of gossip. I've even heard that General Grenville Dodge is
thinking about resigning as Chief Engineer. I heard he got the
job after Peter Dey resigned in 1864 as Chief Engineer because
he was upset about inflated construction bills sent to the
Union Pacific from the Credit Mobilier whose stockholders
then pocketed the difference between the inflated cost and
the actual cost."

Jack Casement sat in stoney silence and in a strained
voice said, "General Dodge is an honorable man, sir."

"Well, I just heard that his wife owned stock in the Credit
Mobilier. And furthermore, that Oakes Ames felt that
President Lincoln ordained that he, Oakes Ames, complete
the railroad. Of course, it was his good fortune that he owned
a shovel manufacturing firm and he could sell the shovels and
other tools they made to the Credit Mobilier at an inflated
price." Charles Richfield paused to look out the window.
"This damn railroad is splitting the country, general. Just
like it's splitting that buffalo herd. It's dividing young Indian
against old as sure as the Missouri Compromise divided slave
state against free state and led to the Civil War."

"Sergeant, I admire a man who isn't afraid to state his
beliefs! I can tell you, with conviction, that General Grant
will be president come November and that he will soon be
meeting with General Dodge at Fort Sanders in Wyoming
Territory to straighten out just one such problem as you've
been discussing. General's Sheridan, Harney, Sherman and
Potter will all be in his party at Fort Sanders. This railroad

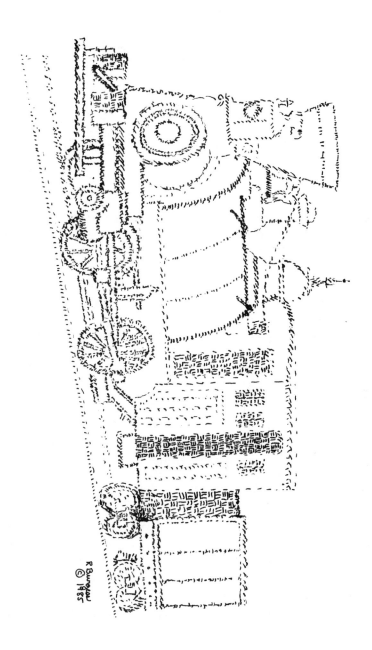

will be built, but it will cost a lot of money. Many will profit.
Many will die. But, I can assure you that the men who work
for me earn their pay. Now, if you will excuse me, I'll go see
if I can't get this damn train moving! Good day, sir."

When the track had reached Cheyenne last year, its
population had grown to 10,000 almost overnight. Charles
had been there and had watched the vigilantes hang several
men. The army post at Fort Russell tried to keep the peace,
to no avail.

Laramie City wasn't any better. Only sixty days old, and
lawlessness ruled the day. That marvelous Dale Creek Bridge
was 136 feet high and 650 feet long; its engineering genius
was testimony to man's potential, but Laramie City was
proof of his wickedness. On the third day as the train stopped
to take on wood and water at Laramie City, the vigilantes'
work was evident on a telegraph pole not fifty feet from
the long newly-built two story train station. A rowdy gambler
dressed in a white shirt with a black and white striped vest
and a flat crowned black hat lying at his feet was hanging,
quite dead.

Ahead lay Fort Sanders like a suburb at the south edge
of town. Four companies of troops had recently been sent to
End of Track at the Platte River to a new garrison to be
named Fort Steele. They would stay on the east bank of the
river while the crew constructed the bridge. Meanwhile,
a ferry would service men and equipment across the Platte.

Charles, descending the steps of the train, brushed the
alkali dust from his blue silk suit and marveled at the huge
windmill that pumped water into the storage tank. Charles
Richfield was a man of average height and weight, he had a
small waist, and heavy arms.

Walking to the baggage car, he retrieved the trunk he had
brought with him to the End of Track. He carried his recently
purchased 1866 Winchester .44 rimfire in its thick steer hide
scabbard. A heavy pair of saddle bags carried mostly ammuni-

tion for his rifle and side arms. He preferred the 1862 Colt Pocket Navy Revolver in .36 caliber because of its mere 4½ inch barrel that rode comfortably in a shoulder holster under his coat. It had a casehardened frame, hammer and lever, but the barrel was blue and the brass gripstraps plated with silver. On the cylinder was engraved a roll scene that depicted the Battle of the Republic of Texas versus the Mexican fleet dated May 16, 1843. A four barreled Sharps .22 rimfire short fired by a revolving firing pin, he carried under his shirt and vest on his right side for a left hand draw. A second gun, a .41 Philadelphia Deringer, he carried in his left boot. At the next stop by the river he would change to his work clothes.

Downtown Laramie City was alive with construction activity. A cloudless sky and hot sun accented the vastness of this mountain plain. Laid out on the east side of the Laramie River, an ample water supply for these huge wood burning steam locomotives was ready at hand. But this wasn't just a watering hole for locomotives. Freight wagons stacked with building materials and waiting to be unloaded jammed the streets and blocked traffic. Angry muleskinners cracked their whips and cursed obstreperously at mules, horses and a few oxen. A cacophony of sounds from barking dogs, the multitude of saloons with men and women laughing, banjos playing, carpenters nailing up battens on tall board false fronts, all competed with the gusting winds coming out of the west. All this noise made Charles want to get off the street.

FREUND & BRO. GUNS, PISTOLS, AMMUNITION.
RIFLES & SHOT GUNS MADE TO ORDER.

Charles read the sign and stepped inside to see row after row of fine rifles and shotguns. A Sharps buffalo rifle caught his eye. "That's a work of art. Fine checkering on the walnut stock. Tasteful engraving on the receiver and slant breech block. .52 caliber. 26 inch barrel," he noticed. "I'll take it and 200 rounds of linen cartridges. I need 500 rounds of .44 rimfire and that pair of field glasses."

The sun was higher when he walked out of the gunshop and crossed the street. A pile of sand, used in construction blocked the traffic of horses and men. Some tough looking women here, but the men aren't too respectable looking either. "If it gets any worse on down the line, we might just as well spend the whole damn summer in the desert," he thought.

Observing the bustle of activity and tons and tons of supplies stacked in staging areas for future needs as he walked along the streets of this new town he hopped back on the train to begin the last leg to Brownsville.

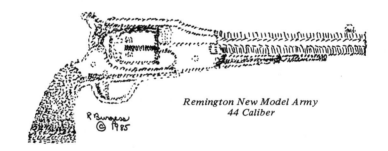

Remington New Model Army
44 Caliber

CHAPTER SEVEN

THE GOLDEN BELLE

Back in 1861, during the early months of the Civil War, Amy had been strangely excited. Glorious reports of southern victories, handsome and dashing officers exuding confidence — it was almost unbearable for an eighteen-year-old New Orleans girl.

She had met Brit Hampton at an Officers' Ball when she was introduced to him by her father, Major General Bruce Stafford. Brit was just a lieutenant, but all the women of New Orleans knew he would go far in politics after the war. Their husbands had reported that he had travelled through Europe in pursuit of his passion for gambling and women.

Amy felt fortunate in having an early dance on her card, for he was a striking dancer. She felt secure because her gown was breath-taking. Now she noticed that he couldn't take his eyes off her as she danced several dances with other young southern officers. She had long black hair exquisitely coiffured. Her dark eyes sparkled under long black lashes, and her low cut bodice revealed a fresh young form of early womanhood.

After the dance many weeks passed with Amy Stafford coyly tantalizing Brit with her seeming disinterest in him, but Brit had made up his mind. "Amy, you're beautiful. You must marry me. You must. I won't take 'no' for an answer."

"Brit, darling. There's a war raging. What kind of life would we have with you off fighting and me here in New Orleans?"

"The war will be over in a few weeks, Amy. The Yankee's are taking a licking. They haven't the stomach for this fight."

They were married in the spring of 1861 after several short months of courtship, which included grande balls and parties in New Orleans high society. They spent huge amounts of money and gambled along the Mississippi during a thirty-day honeymoon. Amy's favorite spot on the river was Natchez, where she purchased several pieces of French Provincial furniture. Brit spoiled her in the extreme. Brit had been born in Natchez and had moved to New Orleans with his family at the age of sixteen. He had traveled extensively in Europe during an eighteen month period, and returned to New Orleans in September of 1859. Then he had entered, without enthusiasm, his father's import business. With the outbreak of hostilities, he eagerly accepted a lieutenacy in one of Louisianas' finest cavalry regiments.

Tragically Brit was killed near Shiloh, the bloodiest battle yet fought in the war. Amy's dislike of the war turned to bitter hatred after Brit's death. She found herself sequestered at home, unwilling to go out, even at her father's insistence. She grew pale and thin, her eyes grew dull. Her father worried about her, tried to hide it, but couldn't. "Amy, you must eat!" he kept imploring her.

The unthinkable began recurring in her dreams, "What if the South should lose?" Her father had gone to the western front near Vicksburg; her mother had died of cholera that year. Now she was totally alone.

Lose they did and by then she had lost everything: Brit at Shiloh, father at Vicksburg, mother with cholera and with it many tears and a sheltered life. Nothing was left but a small hoard of coins and advice about her beauty and talents generously offered by all three so many happy days ago.

She had wisely saved a small hoard of gold coins to purchase a gambling casino and saloon in New Orleans after the war. It might not be the most respectable investment, but she had to be self-sufficient. She spent hours and hours thinking about what lavish gambling casinos should look like. She envisioned high cathedral ceilings with crystal light fixtures sparkling gaily in harmony with thousands of tiny mirrors inlaid in massive Roman columns bordering each side of the long gaming hall.

Every night and into the early morning light Amy's casino hummed with the excitement of people, men and women, elbow to elbow, seeking to escape the memories of the recent war. Instinctively Amy catered to their desires. She provided liquor inexpensively and saw to it that New Orleans' women were welcome guests at her gaming tables. She was generous with those in need, down on their luck, or destitute, but she learned early of the wisdom of firmness with those who would bully, bluff or attempt violence. She stationed armed guards, highly visible, throughout the casino. Most who knew her loved her. None who met her left without a lasting impression. She had made her decision. She would garner all her monetary and physical resources toward a new investment toward the precarious future. With renewed enthusiasm she regained the sparkle in her eyes. Sparkle lost after months of suffering in a war that had taken everything from her that she loved.

By 1865 the South was in ruins; especially those areas in the path of Sherman's troops. General Sherman had begun his penetration of the deep South at Chattanooga and moved south along the railway to Atlanta, burning everything in his

path. Severe shortages of even the barest necessities of life
were commonplace. Near famine faced people daily. The
banking system was in chaos. Now "Reconstruction" was the
Northern cry, and the defeated South was struggling to
comply. The Radical Republicans would have their "pound
of flesh," Especially now that President Lincoln had been
assassinated and replaced by the ineffective new president,
Andrew Johnson. While Lincoln had enunciated the Emanci-
pation Proclamation in 1863, its edict applied only to those
areas under Confederate control. Thus, the Thirteenth
Amendment was proposed which would prohibit slavery
throughout the United States. It stated: "Neither slavery nor
involuntary servitude, except as a punishment for crime
whereof the party shall have been duly convicted, shall
exist within the United States, or any place subject to their
jurisdiction." But three-fourths of the states must ratify
to pass the amendment. Obviously, some of the readmitted
Southern states must vote in favor. While Congress was in
recess, Johnson effectively began a Reconstruction program
whereby Southern states were readmitted after promising to
abolish slavery, repealing the Ordinances of Secession, and
refusing to recognize the Confederate war debt. After
Congress reconvened, the Republicans, with Radical control,
were furious. President Johnson was now the enemy. Congress
set up a Joint Committee on Reconstruction. And, of course,
they needed to study the special problems of the defeated
South. The Negro still did not have citizenship. While
Johnson was supportive of the abolishment of slavery he,
nevertheless, vetoed the Civil Rights Bill which would confer
citizenship to the Negro. That proposal was the central
theme of the Radical's Reconstruction purpose. The measure
was repassed over Johnson's veto, and the stage set for the
Fourteenth Amendment and the bitter prelude to the Radical
leaders' attempt to remove President Johnson from office by
impeachment. But, the President would need to be convicted

of: "Treason, Bribery, or other high Crimes and Misdemeanors." Nevertheless, the Radicals would try to remove Johnson from office. After all, they were instrumental in establishing five military districts throughout the South whose Federal occupation troops assured compliance with the Radical efforts of Reconstruction.

Still, the Federal Troops had spent their Yankee dollars throughout the South. One of the favorite places in New Orleans now was Amy Stafford Hampton's "Golden Belle Casino." She had had no trouble purchasing her property and materials with gold.

Tired soldiers, looking for escape from war's deprivation at Amy's new casino found an atmosphere of excitement and festivity.

Amy saw a magnetically handsome man come into the casino early that evening. Dressed in his major's uniform; he was impressive, "Six feet two inches, two hundred twenty pounds, about thirty-five," she guessed.

"Where are you from, major?" she asked.

"Indiana, Madam."

"Been in New Orleans long?"

"Three or four months."

"May I buy you a drink?"

"I would be delighted," he grinned.

"Sam, the best in the house for the gentleman."

"My name is Amy Stafford," she said; "I own this place."

"I'm Howard Prescott, Miss Stafford. I see you like gambling."

"I enjoy gold, Mr. Prescott. I trust you will leave a little of yours here," she smiled.

"I'm sure I will," he laughed.

The major was fond of poker, but he played roulette because the exciting and lovely owner seemed to spend much of her time around the roulette table. Their eyes met. The major blushed but boldly held her gaze. "Even without the lovely gown she would be the center of attention at any gathering. She is the most beautiful woman I've ever seen," he thought.

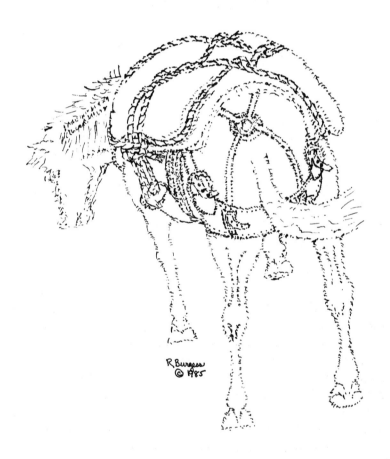

CHAPTER EIGHT

THE YOUNG LIEUTENANT

The 1867 Christmas season in New Orleans found Lieutenant Clark Sampson homesick. His United States Federal Troops regiment had been sent as occupation forces to enforce the Radicals' programs. Clark, as a young lieutenant with Sherman at the end of the war, had hoped to return home to Ohio. After he had spent six months in Atlanta and had watched the painful rebuilding of that city, orders came for duty in New Orleans. Now he was serving out the last of his enlistment and trying to decide whether to re-enlist for duty with the cavalry in the West. Having heard of the quiet charm of New Orleans' famous gambling casino, he had stopped by for a relaxing evening. When he had been there before to check the reports, he had only caught a glance of her. She seemed so busy and he thought, "No time for a lieutenant," as he perused the rich assortment of the crowd. Then, without a look of suspicion or without a moment's hesitation, she had turned him down for a hand of poker.

The "Golden Belle" gambling parlor, with its extravagant

furnishings, imported whiskies, fine wines, lovely ladies, generous gaming tables and exhilarating gaiety shined even brighter in the eyes of Clark after he met its beautiful hostess for the first time. He had been trying to meet her for several weeks, but had been unsuccessful until tonight. For this time, as an introduction he offered, "May I buy you a drink, Ma'am?"

"Sure, soldier. Having any luck?"

"Not until now," he grinned. "I understand you run this place."

"I own it; that's right."

"You married?"

The color briefly left her face as she lost her composure, "My husband was killed at Shiloh, lieutenant."

"I'm sorry," he said sincerely. "I was at Lookout Mountain and then Atlanta."

"My name is Amy Stafford. What's yours young lieutenant?"

"Call me, Clark — Clark Sampson." He looked straight into her eyes and said, "I wonder if you'd have dinner with me? I need to know about you and New Orleans and you need to know about what's north of New Orleans."

She liked his dark, curly hair and the neatly trimmed moustache. "I'm much too busy, Mr. Sampson. The evening shift is coming on."

"More the reason to take a break. We'll go down to the river front and have some seafood. The wine at the wharf is the best in the world," he implored.

"You make it sound devine, lieutenant, and I would like to hear about the North. I'll accept. But let me check on several matters and then let me get my things."

She disappeared into the back of the noisy casino for what seemed like an hour and reappeared in a stunning floor-length white gown with tiny pink sequins. Now her dark hair shown in long curls. "I hope I didn't keep you waiting too long, Lieutenant," she teased.

He stood admiringly, "My carriage is waiting, ma'am."
Outside, the doorman assisted them into the coach, closing
the door after them. "Have a good evening, ma'am." Turning
to Sampson he added, "Sir."

They passed along busy streets filled with people hurrying
about their early evening business. Sunset had long passed
and many restaurants, saloons, and theaters were beginning
to fill up. French architecture and French decor was evident
everywhere. "Chateau la Perriere," called out the driver,
while the footman opened the door of the coach. Stepping
down, Amy took Clark's arm and he escorted her into the
dimly lighted, but elegantly decorated establishment.

"Madame, Monsieur, good evening." announced the
maitre d'. Seating them at a candle-lighted table covered
with an exquisite silk cloth he offered, "Monsieur, may I
suggest "Chateaux Margaux" to tease the palate?" He waited
politely.

"Magnifique." Clark replied.

Carefully, the maitre d' drew the cork, and just as deftly
decanted the wine past a gently flickering candle, into a
carafe. This pleasantly sensuous ritual continued while he
poured a small portion into a crystal goblet and handed it
to Clark. Amy watched while Clark tasted the red wine.

"Marvelous." exclaimed Clark.

"Ah." beamed the maitre d' as he poured for both of them.
"Enjoy your dinner."

An appetizer of small fillets of poached perch garnished
with Beurre Blanc L'Ermitage sauce whose ivory colored
surface sparkled in the candle light was the precursor of the
elegant meal that followed. On a chilled plate the waiter
brought Coeur A La Creme with shiny beads of red and black
caviar on each side of the plate.

"His prediction was right. This is excellent wine; I must be
sure my casino has some of his shipment," thought Amy
before she said, "Clark, I must congratulate you. This is a

splendid French restaurant. You have good taste in many things. Tell me about yourself."

"I was in college when the war broke out. I was just finishing my second year in architecture. My first thought after seeing your casino was that a talented architect must have designed it."

A pistachio studded mousseline graced with a velonté sauce was accented by the exquisitely dry Pouilly-Fumé wine.

"I'm sure you will make a fine architect. Do you plan to return to college?"

"My parents want me to return to France to finish my studies. They took me to Europe where we lived in several countries for nearly two years. I learned French, or at least how to get by in the language. I studied German for several months. Mother wants me to finish my education, preferably in France. I'm afraid I've disappointed her. I'm going to serve one more tour of duty in the army."

"My father was killed in the war," Amy said, "I know how your mother must feel about your choice. I have only heartache and pain to remind me of things military."

"You are much too beautiful to be unhappy, Amy. I am the one who is sad for having to leave New Orleans after having just met you.'

"Forgive me, Clark, for my moment of remorse. I don't know what came over me. You, of course, should pursue your career by doing whatever pleases you. I admire that quality in a man. Tell me, where did you come by your expertise and good taste in gourmet dining?"

He grinned, "My mother. She loves to cook. She and father took me to many fine restaurants in Europe. It has become one of my passions. You could easily become another."

Amy blushed, "I have enjoyed myself tonight, Clark. You have made me forget. Now tell me, where will you be assigned?"

"Fort John Buford in Dakota Territory. There is talk

that country will become Wyoming Territory and the Fort will be renamed Fort Sanders."

"Oh, that sounds so exciting. I have heard so much about the frontier. My father talked about it constantly. Wagon trains, blizzards, buffalo, gold mining camps and Indians. Are there still Indians in that area?" she asked, with the flush of adventure in her face.

"Not many at End of Track, but this time last year Red Cloud began his attacks on the forts along the Bozeman Trail. Now the Indians attack grading parties and small survey parties far ahead of the completed railroad tracks. Engineers are still trying to cross the Black Hills just west of Cheyenne at Dale Creek. The chief engineer named it Sherman Hill."

"That should be a tough hill then, shouldn't it, Lieutenant?" All southerners hated Sherman because he had burned his way through the South. "War is Hell!" he said and did his part to make it so.

Clark caught her meaning about Sherman, but chose to ignore it, "The Indians and outlaws attack freight lines and mining camps, especially in the Sweetwater Country, but I've heard the miners are taking huge amounts of gold out of there."

"Gold has been one of my hobbies, Clark," she smiled as the sparkle of her eyes rested on him as he rose to help her from her chair.

The fragrance of her perfume was intoxicating as he sat close to her in the gently swaying carriage. The warmth of her shoulder and the fullness of her thigh excited him. He reached for her hand and she didn't refuse him.

"Clark, won't you come up for a brandy?" she asked.

CHAPTER NINE

A RIVER TRIP

Just fifteen hundred miles and Howard would be there. It had taken over three days to reach Council Bluffs from Cheyenne by railroad. But now he could see the two black columns of smoke spewing from the dual smokestacks of the "Out West" streaming behind the 160 foot long riverboat. She was headed down the Missouri toward St. Louis. She could carry 200 tons of freight and had cabins for thirty passengers, but there were twice that many people on the boiler deck alone. The main channel was still clear, but ice was already forming along the banks. He had timed this return trip well and what lay ahead had promise.

New Orleans would be as warm as his desire to see Amy Stafford. She had been on his mind for the past eighteen months since he had first seen her. He had written letters proposing marriage, but she laughed them off with disinterest in her short letters inquiring about his new environment and activities. And now, even though Amy's "Golden Belle" Casino prospered, the nation's economy foundered.

That 'greenback" dollar had taken its toll on the nation's economy. More correctly, the Civil War had taken its toll, for to finance the war, Secretary of the Treasury Chase found the nation's Treasury to be empty in 1861 due largely to the Panic of 1857 and the Tariff Act of 1857 which decreased revenues to the government. Lincoln's administration issued $450 million of treasury notes, known as "greenbacks" paper, unsupported by gold. Chase deprecated this measure, but how was the war to be financed when it was destined to cost billions? Bonds began to sell after battlefield victories for the North became more significant in 1864. Gold and silver was taken out of the banks and hoarded. After the war the treasury ceased issuing greenbacks, but economic expansion continued. Prices fell. Cries of the "Greenback Movement" were being heard by 1868.

He had been at several forts on the Bozeman Trail during 1866. Howard had bought two wagons and started his own business after he had been mustered out of the cavalry. It was then that he went to End of Track and started to freight to mining camps until he had increased his stake. But it was the expansion of freighting all the way to Virginia City, Montana that had led to his wealth. Over a period of twelve months he saw a steady, satisfying growth in the numbers of horses, mules, and wagons in his business.

His own, The Prescott Stage and Freight Line, had grown into an impressive financial venture since he had last seen her. He was getting three dollars per hundred pounds per hundred miles and some of the jerk lines with three or four wagons pulled by ten to twenty mules had paid for themselves in one trip. A good pair of mules brought seven hundred hard American dollars; a good freight wagon cost upwards of one thousand dollars. During those eighteen months he had accumulated four stage coaches and a score of freight wagons. Now he centered much of his activity at South Pass, Wyoming

Territory where he had a line to Fort Bridger and east to
Fort Laramie.

Jefferson Davis was Secretary of War prior to the Civil War
and southern congressmen were effective in getting the
Overland Route staged through Santa Fe, but that trail
was moved north at the outset of the Civil War to deny the
Confederates easy prey along its route. But long before,
when Butterfield had owned the line along the southern
route, the stockholders of that company had prohibited the
carrying of gold and silver because of the tempting nature
toward holdups that resulted by transporting those precious
metals.

When Howard transported gold from the Virginia City,
Montana mines south to the railhead in Cheyenne and later
in Laramie City, he hid it throughout the freight goods
so that even the muleskinners were unaware that it was part
of the cargo. After the Fetterman Massacre the Bozeman
Trail became very dangerous, and Howard slowly pulled his
line back to the Oregon Trail.

Now Howard stood at the lifeline looking at the cold
water below, "This ice could devastate a steamboat," he
thought, as the captains of several vessels had found out two
years ago right here in St. Louis. A severe winter had frozen
the river solid, crushed and totally destroyed dozens of
steamboats tied at the levee.

Even as he disembarked, he noticed that the boardwalk
on the St. Louis waterfront was covered with snow. Here
Howard transferred to a larger Mississippi River steamboat
for the rest of his journey to New Orleans. They had
bypassed several landings on their fast river trip but stopped
occasionally to take on fuel that the wood hawks had
gathered. The prevailing current made the down-river trip
fast and pleasant.

Large amounts of gold dust were being transported by
steamboat. Part of Howard's business in Montana was to

surreptitiously freight gold to the Upper Missouri for further transport to St. Louis. He hadn't liked to ship gold because it had drawn every outlaw in the territory.

While he was in the army, he had spent several months on the Mississippi under less pleasant circumstances. But now he thought only of the bewitching, dark haired owner of a gambling casino. "Beauty such as hers will make a man do strange things," he thought smiling to himself as he remembered the past eighteen months. "I haven't written so many letters in my life."

When he finally arrived at his long-planned destination, New Orleans was experiencing torrential rains. January high waters from tributary streams had made the Mississippi rise to flood stage. Docking under hazardous circumstances required every ounce of strength and river knowledge in this steam captain's book. The levees were jammed with steamboats and smaller craft seeking shelter. Fog horns echoed throughout the delta.

Normally calm and in control of his emotions, the thought of seeing Amy brought a shiver of anticipation through his mind, "Buggy!" he cried through the sheets of heavy rain.

"Where to, boss?" the driver of the two-horse carriage asked.

"The Golden Belle."

"Yes, Suh."

The casino, full of gamblers and soldiers, merchants, seamen and beautiful women, seemed alive with activity as it suddenly struck him that she might not want to give all this up. He panicked as he heard her call his name.

"Howard, darling!" she cried, "I thought you'd never get here." She opened her arms and embraced him while he lifted her off the floor and tenderly kissed her.

"That raging Mississippi was trying to push us right on out into the ocean," said Howard, beaming with excitement.

"You're drenched. Don't just stand here! Come, I'll find you some dry clothing."

They went to her private room in the back where she
opened the double doors of her long wardrobe. On one end,
neatly arranged, were Brit's jackets. She quickly produced
a velvet smoking jacket that was just right for him. "This
belonged to Brit. I haven't disposed of these jackets yet."
She poured him a warming whiskey and then said, "I've
been thinking of your proposal, and I am accepting; however,
I'll need about two months to arrange my affairs here in
New Orleans."

He was stunned. He had expected a prolonged courtship
and an expensive absence from his business, but this was
exhilarating, "I had hoped to take you up river with me."

"I'll have to sell this place, which won't be difficult, but
it will take a little time, darling."

"You won't be sorry, I promise," he said, fidgeting with
a whiskey decanter, "The freight business won't last much
longer what with the railroad due to link up coast to coast
in another year. But I've made all the money a man could
hope for. We'll move to San Francisco, or New York, or
even Europe, or wherever you want, Amy," he said,
nervously in a voice used to self-assurance but now cracking
under the excitement of the unexpected acceptance.

"Oh, we'll have a good life, Howie. Now why don't you
tell me all about freighting and the Indian Country." She
settled herself very close, kissed him lightly on the cheek
and smiled.

Howard took a mouthful of whiskey and swallowed.
"I have wheelrights working for me around the clock to
repair and build all the wheels we need. You'd be surprised
at the number of wheels and axles we go through each week.
And there are enough blacksmiths on the payroll to man
a troop of cavalry. We hitch mules to the lead wagon with
a long, heavy chain extended from the two lead mules to
the wagon. The team nearest the wagon is hitched to the
tongue while all other pairs of mules are attached to the

master chain. We often join three or four wagons. They're coupled together with eight to twelve mules out in front, depending on the terrain and weight of the goods we're hauling. I know of one line up in Montana, that just sold for $75,000. It would have been a good buy, just for the 116 wagons in the lot. But they had no mules — 500 oxen went with it though."

"Do you own any oxen, Howard?"

"No. I prefer horses and mules. Oxen are too slow for my operation. They have their advantages, however. No need for expensive harness, they don't need grain, and they're not as prized by the Indian." He poured Amy a glass of sherry, handed it to her, and kissed her on the mouth.

"You'll like South Pass City, Amy! It's located down in a valley with friendly people and spectacular mountains to the north. My freight and stage line office is headquartered along the main street in a hotel I own. You'll even get to keep your hand in at gambling, if you want, since there's a gambling hall or saloon in about every other building."

They talked well into the night as he explained the answer to her every question of how a jerk line is rigged and how the Indians will shoot the nigh horse first, and then finish off the driver and passengers, "It's a dangerous business," he said, seriously.

"It sounds very exciting. Tell me about the gold."

"Road agents and outlaws are everywhere. We can't carry gold and let anyone know it, not even the driver. So we go to all kinds of trouble to hide it in boxes, even in whiskey barrels. We usually carry at least $10,000 in dust and occasionally up to $200,000. The trains have quit carrying gold for payment of their construction gangs. They pay them in currency. It has decreased the number of holdups, but it has increased the demand from the mines for us to carry it. I don't like it, but it's profitable. We've been held up several times, but so far we haven't lost much."

"Do you have an escort? How many men are there on a freight run? Is there just one wagon out at a time?" she asked, her face flushed from the sherry and the nearness of him, while her dark eyes sparkled in the lamplight.

"Usually two men, ten to twelve mules, two or three wagons, that's about it."

"Doesn't the army help you?"

He laughed, "They're spread so thin, trying to guard the railroad tracklayers, graders and surveyors; and then there is the Oregon Trail, the Overland Trail, and all those mines on the Sweetwater. We probably get four or five troopers every fourth or fifth run we make and then only over the dangerous stretches."

"Well, I'm looking forward to it even if it is dangerous."

"Heavens, you don't think you'll be going on a stage line, do you? My plan is for you to take the riverboat to Council Bluffs and from there to travel by railroad — the Union Pacific — straight down the line to End of Track which should be one hundred to one hundred-fifty miles west of Cheyenne by then." He paused, and then added, "You can keep me posted by telegraph. When you arrive, I'll meet you."

"Oh, Howard. How thoughtful. I hadn't really considered going upriver. My father had gone around the Horn of South America twice and across the Isthmus of Panama once. I have been planning so long to make that trip!" a puckish grin heightened the pleasure of her light kiss to his lips.

For months she had read every account she could find about the opening of the West. She studied the paintings of George Catlin and Alfred Jacob Miller; read and re-read the Journals of Lewis and Clark; listened intently to any and all who patronized her casino if they had traveled, or had talked to anyone who had traveled, west of the Mississippi.

"I will be leaving for San Francisco by ship in February. I already have my ticket. I'll then go by rail through

Sacramento and on to the railhead of the Central Pacific which should let me arrive somewhere around Salt Lake City by June. From there by stage to Fort Bridger and then through South Pass. Just that new word: South Pass. That's where the gold is mined. See, I've done my homework!"

"You certainly have," he said, admiringly. "By then the End of Track from the east should just about have reached the Platte River.

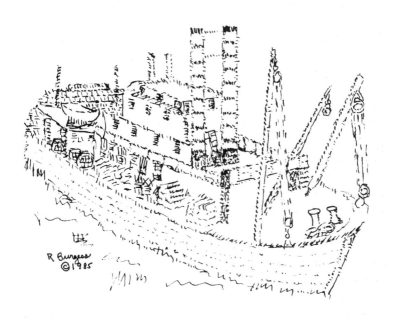

CHAPTER TEN

RATTLESNAKE PASS

The banks of the Medicine Bow River had very few trees, but sagebrush grew tall in draws where it trapped snow during the long winter months. Jimmy knew that the next crossroad in his journey was just ahead as he saw the clumps of cottonwood trees along the river. Following the south fork of this stream, he turned west up a small tributary coming off the north face of Elk Mountain whose heavily timbered slopes remained snow covered much of the year. Jimmy rode through the remains of Fort Halleck, abandoned just two years earlier.

Morning passed while Jimmy approached Rattlesnake Pass. "The right name," he noted, as his horse shied several times after encounters with those nasty creatures. He liked their roasted meat, which reminded him of frog legs, but they still gave him the shivers.

The gradual climb was easy for the bay, and at the summit they stopped for a brief rest before the final leg of the trip. The scout pulled the saddle from the big horse and checked his back for galling. Satisfied with the horse's condition, he turned it loose to graze while he filled a pipe and surveyed the scene below. He could see Pass Creek, with its treeless banks and westerly flowing water that joined the Platte. Overhead, large, white, fluffy coulds, like pillows, drifted rapidly toward the east. "Badlands and desert below. Thousands of square miles. Mostly uninhabited and mostly treeless; mostly windy and mostly dangerous," he surveyed, and then he picked up his pad and saddle and said aloud to the horse, "Let's go see Howie."

Moving rapidly down Pass Creek to its confluence with the Platte, he judged they now had only five more miles to go. He saw the train and the track like a miniature river to the north, its brown smoke easily visible amid a long cloud of reddish brown dust.

"There must be a lot of people milling around down there," he thought, "Those white canvas tents arranged in several rows must be the quarters for the cavalry. Hell, would you look at that bunch of tents on up the river. Half of Laramie City must be there."

The bay sensed the excitement of the place and increased its tempo from a fast walk to a full trot. "No need to urge him along now," Jimmy thought, as the horse found its way through the thick brush along the river. The horse threw its head up, neighed, stopped, and then commenced walking at a slow pace. From a hundred yards downriver came the answering neighs of several horses. Jimmy's horse once more broke into a spirited trot. In a short time Jimmy saw a herder watching several horses grazing along the river bottom.

Now the herder saw Jimmy break out into the open and with a start raised his rifle to the ready. Honoring the open palm of the approaching rider, the herder lowered his rifle. As Jimmy neared, the herder asked, "Seen any Injuns?" with an admiring look at Jimmy's bay.

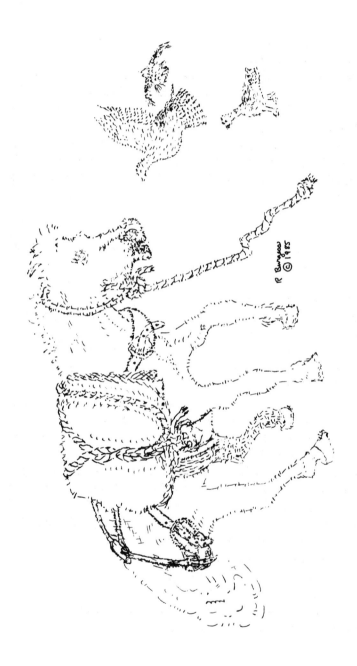

"Not today," said Jimmy. "I had a skirmish with an Arapaho buck yesterday."

The herder offered his plug of tobacco which Jimmy accepted. "What cavalry unit is that on down the river?" asked Jimmy. He took a healthy bite out of the plug and handed it back to the herder.

"G Troop, 2nd Cavalry, Lt. Robinson, commanding. And Co. B, 30th Infantry, Captain Bartlett, commanding," answered the herder. "They've got their hands full just trying to keep order in this place." He spat a stream of tobacco into the dust. "More women arrived last week. Better watch them close. Everyone of them carries a gun in her garter and a knife in her boot. But hell, everything that flies, crawls, walks or runs is armed in this country.

"My name's Jimmy Robineaux. Who you working for?"

"Mr. Prescott, Jimmy. My name's Len Crosswell."

"Much obliged for the tobacco," Jimmy said as he turned the bay down the river.

Later as he neared the first series of tents he asked a man bent over a wooden bucket doing laundry, "You know Howard Prescott?"

The man, dressed in dirty black broadcloth trousers and no shirt, stood up and put his hands to the small of his back and said, as if in pain, "Never heard of him!" Then he promptly went back to his work.

Nearer the tracks he asked a teamster unloading a wagon the same question. "Prescott. I'm looking for Howard Prescott."

"Mr. Prescott's tent is on down by the tracks on this side. He has two tents joined end to end. You can't miss it."

"Thank you," Jimmy said.

"You a friend of Mr. Prescott's?"

"Yes," said Jimmy.

"Too bad about the holdup. I heard all about it," he said and waited for a comment from Jimmy.

"Yea," he said.

Jimmy saw hundreds of tents pitched across sage and sand, like sailboats tossed on a stormy sea. Gusting winds threatened to destroy several hastily erected lean-tos and tents. Choking dust that had gathered quietly in the morning now billowed skyward, fanned by the swirling, sweeping wind.

Jimmy, a light chuckle welling in his throat, thought, "Damn wind. Won't be any tents left to hold this sand down come morning."

CHAPTER ELEVEN

WIND

Charles walked to the end of the rail car to look at an early explorer's map. It showed the Laramie Plains with the surrounding topography. "This area is huge," thought Charles. "Its eastern border is the Black Hills while its western limit is the Medicine Bow Mountains with Elk Mountain as its northern sentinel. At 7,200 feet elevation it is nothing but a high mountain park." He had heard how workers laid track. The more track laid, the more money the Union Pacific made; it was as simple as that, and now the Central Pacific raced across the Nevada desert to join rails with the Union Pacific. Temporary trestles spanned creeks and gullies while permanent bridges waited later construction. Thus the narrow ribbon of rail surged across vast wastelands, mountain gorges, rivers and desert. Once the engineers bridged Dale Creek just to the east of Laramie City, the race ran to the North Platte River. Crews cut tens of thousands of ties and floated them down numerous creeks and streams to the Platte where tie hacks stacked them along the railroad siding and loaded them aboard flatcars.

The train had stopped for two hours for wood and water at Medicine Bow and during that time Charles counted four log buildings, a freight wagon with its team of six mules, and several riding horses. "There are more dogs than people," he noted.

Charles impatiently paced up and down along side the passenger coach in the intense heat. "I can't remember wind so fierce," he thought.

"All aboard!" called the conductor.

"Does the wind always blow like this?" Charles asked a young fellow manning the water spout on the huge water tank.

"Every damn day," he said, cheerfully. "The wind kind of grows on you. One minute you don't see it — the next minute — pow! Like that locomotive hit you."

"How long have you been here?"

"Four weeks," he replied.

The train started moving as Charles stepped onto the ladder. Soon the train was traveling at a fast pace of twenty miles an hour. They would be there soon. Now as he looked at the approaching scenery, he could see the cottonwoods first, and then the tents strung out for half-a-mile up the river. The train slowed to enter the quarter mile wye where switches would allow it to back onto the main track, headed the way it had come.

"Brownsville, folks," said the train conductor. "End of Track. Platte River. Watch your step, ladies."

As Charles stepped from the train, he noticed stacks of boxes and sacks of grain and flour, whiskey barrels and ties, rails and timbers strewn for several hundred yards down the tracks.

On a siding stood the construction train with its boxcars full of bunks for the workers. On top of the boxcars were tents pitched for sleeping. Flatcars bulged with rails and ties.

A long haystack, fenced with poles, swarmed with workers busily loading loose hay onto a large freight wagon.

Charles went back to the baggage car to retrieve his trunk. The trunk, loaded at Omaha, was heavy. A handler lifted it to the ground and left it. Charles looked around for help and there was none. "Howie should be here somewhere," he thought. He started walking toward the main row of tents and noted the number of services available. Restaurants, boarding houses, bath houses, and every other tent a saloon or gambling parlor. A sign on one tent stated: LAUNDRY $1.00 — FORTUNES TOLD $1.00. Down the river he saw the military tents. They were only slightly more orderly.

Suddenly, Charles saw him. Howard, bent intently over a map, looked up at the sound of Charles' footsteps. "Charles! Good to see you." Howard said, shaking his hand. "Did you have a good trip?"

"I enjoyed it, Howard. It was my first trip over that Dale Creek bridge. That was frightening." Charles looked around and saw the horses. "All these horses yours?"

"No, but let's see if we can't find one for you," he said, while walking down the tracks toward a large corral full of horses and mules.

"From the sound of your telegram, it was obvious that you had a good deal of trouble a few days ago. Anymore news?"

"I'll give you the details in the tent. Pick out your mount. I've got our packmules selected. They're in that pen at the end of the corral. They all have fresh shoes and are ready to travel. Jimmy's waiting for us down at the tent, and I expect Jedediah in shortly."

For several long moments, Charles took in a comprehensive view of his surroundings. "This sure isn't like Fort Reno, is it, Major?"

"No," Howard laughed. "They call this place, Brownsville. Percy Brown was a fine man, a good officer, and a good surveyor. He took an arrow in the gut." Howard turned toward the west and pointed, "Brown was sixty miles from here, and fifteen miles north of the head of Bitter Creek." He turned again, faced the tents, and once more swept his hand across the panorama. "This place isn't much of a legacy."

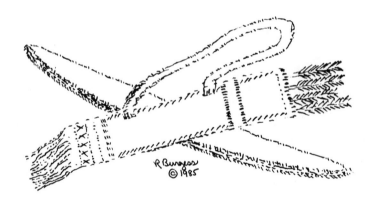

CHAPTER TWELVE

A LONG JOURNEY

Without looking back she had left the Deep South for adventure in the West. Selling the "Golden Belle" had been a simple matter. Howard had no more than boarded the riverboat before Amy took payment in gold and deposited it in New Orleans' most respected bank.

She wanted so much to see San Francisco. Stories of the Gold Rush and tales of gambling and gala parties along the city's famous sea port attracted her with an allure that made her heart race as she boarded the sail rigged, sidewheeler steamship. Its one large mast forward and a smaller aft, was skillfully trimmed by the boatswain and his crew. The route from New Orleans to San Francisco was south for ten days to Panama where the passengers transferred across the Isthmus by railroad to a waiting ship on the Pacific side for further transport to San Francisco. Prior to 1855, when the railroad cars rolled across the Isthmus of Panama, travelers found it necessary to portage across Panama by boat on the Chagres River and by mule train. A wealthy ship operator,

Cornelius Vanderbilt, used a Nicaragua portage in 1851 rather than the Panama crossing.

Famous clipper ships, three-masted vessels like the FLYING CLOUD, whose yard-arms carried thousands of square feet of canvas were disappearing from the scene to be replaced by steamships. Even though less glamorous, adventurers eagerly booked passage aboard ships like the JAVA BEAUTY whose holds bulged at dock-side when Amy got off the train.

A few minutes later Amy boarded the ship where the captain met her.

"Welcome aboard, ma'am. Have a pleasant journey. If I may be of assistance, please let me know." he bowed politely and squeezed her hand. She sensed his immediate interest.

Amy nodded her head and said, "Thank you, Captain."

Two days later, the Captain insisted that she dine with him in the Officer's Mess each evening. He had quite good taste for wines and liquors because he had collected the best from around the world during his many worldwide voyages aboard the JAVA BEAUTY. Fine silverware and china with cutglass crystal accented the gourmet meals the European cooks provided for the Captain's beautiful guest.

At the weekly Captain's Ball handsome women in charming gowns gossiped in small groups about the Captain's lady with the dark eyes and soft white skin. "She's a senator's wife," said one. "I've heard she has millions," said another. "Yes, she made it off poor southern soldiers!" joined a third.

"May I have this dance, Miss Amy?"

"Why of course, Captain."

He was a rather stout man who carried himself very gracefully about the floor. All the women who watched the captain and his beautiful partner smiled their approval in an ingratiating manner.

"I have been in every country in the world, and I have not seen such a beauty as you," he said, matter-of-factly.

"Captain, you do tease, don't you?"

"To the contrary, I have not been able to think of anything else since I first saw you board my ship."

She liked to feel his strong arms about her but knew that to encourage him might be unwise.

"Well, Captain, I hope that I have made your trip a happy one."

"Immensely, my dear, but it's not over yet. Won't you join me for a private party later? A small group of friends will be in my cabin for cards."

"But of course, Captain; however, I will need to freshen up."

"I'll escort you from your cabin. I'll be by in an hour."

The Captain's quarters sparkled in teak and mahogany gathered from the South Seas and inlaid in bas relief of silver, gold and ivory. A string quartet provided soothing melodies. Four other guests were sipping drinks and laughing when they arrived.

"Ladies and gentlemen, may I present Miss Amy Stafford."

Formal introductions followed, and for a moment Amy thought this might be a most boring party until she realized that the card game was to be poker.

"I'm not very good at this game, Captain," she whispered softly.

He smiled graciously and offered her a chair.

"Rather lavish game," she noted. Twenty dollar gold pieces were the smallest denomination on the table.

"Will you accept my note, Captain? I hadn't thought to bring money.

"Of course, my lovely," he chortled, pushing two thousand dollars in gold coin in front of her.

"Five card stud, ladies and gentlemen, five card stud," announced their host.

The Captain painstakingly opened a new deck of cards and deftly fan spread them face up on the table for all to inspect. Pleased with his performance, he proclaimed to the group, "One of life's small pleasures is the game of poker. Wouldn't you agree, Miss Stafford?"

"When it's played for gold, Captain, it's more than just pleasure."

"And, my dear, what do you find intriguing about gold?" coyly asked one of the women.

"Owning it. Lots of it," she smiled.

After about an hour Amy's stack had dwindled to about fifteen hundred dollars.

"Freshen your drink, Miss Amy?" offered the stewart.

"Yes, please do."

Several in the group had been drinking rather heavily, and she knew it was time to become more bold.

"And I'll raise four hundred," she said.

The lovely poker player had a pair of trey's back-to-back.

"She's paired up," one of the ladies exclaimed, shaking her head knowingly.

"I'm out."

"Me too."

With bets and raises the pot swelled to at least five thousand dollars at the turn of the fifth card.

She caught her third trey.

"Five hundred," she said coolly.

Two treys were showing. She had everyone beat except the Captain who had a possible ace high straight. He needed a queen.

"And I'll raise you a thousand," he grinned.

The other two players dropped out.

"Call your thousand," she paused, "and raise you five thousand, Captain."

He wasn't grinning now. "You only have two thousand on the table." She nodded, a faint smile at the corners of her mouth. "You'll advance me another three thousand, Captain?" He studied her cards for a few seconds, and then pushed his five thousand to the center of the table and turned over an ace in the hole.

She smiled coquettishly and turned over her third trey.

"That's enough for me," agreed everyone at the table.

"Goodnight, Captain," the guests said as they left the cabin.

"Well, Miss Amy, you were quite lucky tonight. May I pour you a drink?"

"Thanks, I would like a brandy."

"Tell me, what are your plans when you reach San Francisco?"

"I'll be traveling on to Sacramento in about a month."

"In that case, I insist that you stay in my home after we arrive. You will be near all the gaity of a busy, exciting city."

"Oh, I can't accept, Captain. You are much too kind. I do thank you for your thoughtfulness."

His vanity frustrated, he tried again, "But, Amy, darling. I have such a large, fine home, and I'll be leaving for the South Pacific in two weeks." He saw persistence in her eyes and stammered, "Amy, dear, I would like to see you . . . I . . ."

"Captain, I will be staying in a hotel. If you'd like, I'll be happy to accompany you to dinner. I do so enjoy the opera." She looked teasingly at him while a pout hinted at the corners of her lips.

After the bustle of arrival and details of seeing to their trunks and boxes, they had a marvelous time for the two weeks they were together in San Francisco. He fell madly in love with her and spent vast amounts of money trying to lure her into marrying him. He took her to the dressmakers for clothes suitable for travel and life on the frontier.

While she modeled a colorful plaid riding costume, he asked, "Amy, why are you going to the mountains?"

"I am going to marry Howard Prescott."

Stunned, he sat silently; the color drained from his face. "And I can't change your mind?"

"No, my dear Captain. I have enjoyed San Francisco, its

lovely bay, the opera, your company and your friendship,
but I must be on my way."

Sacramento was a quiet town. It had a more western
appearance, but still there were many brick and adobe
buildings with red clay-tiled roofs. Board sided, false fronted
stores lined its streets and there was an occasional log
cabin. Amy made a special trip to the Central Pacific
Railroad depot where she sent a telegraph to:

FORT SANDERS. LARAMIE CITY.
WYOMING TERRITORY.
LIEUTENANT CLARK SAMPSON. STOP
WILL LEAVE SOUTH PASS END OF JUNE.
STOP AMY

The message sent, she looked around for a women's
clothier. Her wardrobe needed several additions, particularly
her travel clothing. By train to End of Track, gowns would
be appropriate for travel, but for travel by stagecoach she
would need more comfortable apparel. She tried on several
items; none pleased her.

"Much too drab, my dear." she said to the shop-owner.
"I had something colorful in mind, something exciting."
She walked down the aisle of bolted cloth and selected
several bolts of different materials, including silk, wool,
gingham woven in stripes, checks, and plaids, lustrously
finished broadcloth with a tight twill weave, and lace woven
of silk. "I am going into the desert. I have no idea when I
will return to civilization. The desert may be dreary, but I
don't intend to be."

"Yes, Madam, I understand," said the owner, anxiously.
She motioned to her tailor who appeared quickly with an
assistant. The tailor, in his sixties, thin, balding, whose beak
nose supported silver rimmed glasses, bowed slightly.

"I like these materials," Amy continued. "You may use
them freely," she instructed. "Full skirts, pleated to cover

leggings to allow for horseback riding in comfort. Gowns with matching hats. I particularly like large hats with lots of lace. Several costumes tailored with matching short waist-length vests."

"Such beauty and such a figure." said the tailor admiringly. "I am sure you will be pleased with our discriminating portfolio, Madam. We will have sketches ready by 3:00 o'clock tomorrow afternoon. Our dressmakers and seamstresses will work overtime to complete m'lady's wardrobe expeditiously."

"You are most kind," Amy acknowledged. "I shall look forward to see the sketches. Good afternoon."

"Good afternoon, Madam," the owner replied.

The following days passed quickly while Amy shopped for western accoutrements, items she thought necessary for the dry, high mountain desert. A Remington Vest Pocket Deringer, palm sized, struck her as a practical addition to her belongings. A second gun, a Remington Double Deringer in .41 caliber jostled in her shoulder bag. Firearms were not foreign to her education, for her father taught her the use of weapons during her early childhood. "The pistol, Amy, is like any other tool." he had said, "Learn to use it skillfully."

Down the street the hardware store owned by Collis Huntington and Mark Hopkins, headquartered the Central Pacific line. Amy watched curiously at the bustle of activity in and out of the establishment. The Big Four of the C.P., Leland Stanford, president; C.P. Huntington, vice president; Mark Hopkins, treasurer; and Charles Crocker, president of the construction company, formed the race eastward to join with the rails of the westbound Union Pacific. One successful decision was to form the Contract and Finance Company with Charles Crocker as president. Similar to the Credit Mobilier, this company garnered millions into the laps of the Big Four.

The street led to Sacramento's train depot which clanged

with activity as she boarded for the eastern journey over the Sierra Mountains. The train stopped frequently for wood and water as it labored up steep grades and slowly negotiated narrow, dangerous canyons as it traveled from California's western slopes to Nevada. On this train every passenger had a deck of cards, most of them marked. Just the way she liked it. The sharpies all took her for easy pickens, but her attractiveness deceived them.

"I suggest you find a sucker, mister," she said as she raked in a stack of gold coins, "You dog-ear cards in my neck of the woods and you'd get shot."

"You sayin' I'm a cheat?" asked the nattily dressed card sharp.

"No, just a fool," she smiled. "Good day."

Looking out the train window it thrilled her to realize that the Carson City, Nevada mint with its fabulous exhibit of gold dust and nuggets, some as big as a coffee cup, was her next stop. She planned to spend a few days there, resting and sightseeing.

The United States Mint, an imposing stone, square two-story building of great character, fascinated her. Equally impressive, was the huge stack of silver bullion bars, as big as a giant loaf of bread. They would become the famous Carson City silver dollar.

From Carson City to Virginia City, just twenty miles to the northeast, work had started on a railroad, but was not completed, so Amy rode by stagecoach over a rugged road to Virginia City, Nevada. In New Orleans, she had heard of the famous Comstock Lode; now she was going to see it. The contrast between the two cities was evident. Carson City had many churches. Virginia City boasted of fifty gambling saloons and one church. She would not have time to visit either. Enormous amounts of gray silver-bearing ore had already come from this mine, but Amy's passion was gold. She stayed overnight in a rowdy hotel where every-other man was drunk and every woman occupied.

The following day she traveled back to Carson City by stage where she reboarded the train for the five-hundred-mile trip to Salt Lake City. "I'd like to tarry here; but South Pass beckons."

Her bewitching manner gathered men to her table in every car. Games of three card monte and poker helped her pass the time traveling through the desolate Humboldt Desert. The few springs along the way attracted the emigrant trains before the railroad and had become the center for trade and supply. Here there were just stops for the train. Intriguing names like Winnemucca, Golconda, Palisade and Wells; names thought up by land promoters and published in gaudy exaggeration belied the promise of riches and wealth. Most likely there were outlaws, Indians and death.

Three days later the train reached End of Track, still fifty miles from Salt Lake City. Here, manpower, horsepower, and wagons did the day's work. Far ahead, into the evening light, workers laid rough hewed ties and spiked rails into place. Amy stepped from the train into the alkali dust of the desert and looked around for assistance. She saw her baggage, stacked in a pile, alongside the baggage car. "Driver!" she called, "Will you be so kind as to assist me with my things?"

"My goodness, lady, what are you going to do with all them trunks? I ain't got room on my stage for all that stuff," said a crusty old stage driver with tobacco juice stains in his beard.

"Oh, my dear man, I must have all these things if I am to go into this savage country!"

"Probably none of us 'l git thar if'n my horses have to pack all that stuff along," he mumbled as he stacked the stage high with Amy's trunks and hat boxes.

In a few minutes she was on her way. A Mormon farmer

and his wife were the only other passengers on the long dry trail into Salt Lake City. The trip would take fourteen hours with two changes of horses along the way. It was choking hot and dirty. Amy listened politely while the farmer told her of the beauty and majesty of Salt Lake City and the Wasatch Mountains. He described the method of construction of the Tabernacle, how ox cart teams had pulled huge wagons loaded with one block of granite at a time. The granite blocks, used to build the Temple, weighed up to five tons each and posed a laborious task to the dedicated workers.

During Amy's two day rest in Salt Lake City she learned of the 1857 Mountain Meadows Massacre. Three hundred-fifty miles from Salt Lake City, Mountain Meadows was the site of the massacre of 120 emigrants, the victims of Mormon wrath after Buchanan had replaced Brigham Young as governor of Utah Territory with a non-Mormon from Georgia named Alfred Cumming. Trouble enough had faced President James Buchanan during 1857 with the impending Civil War and the infamous Dred Scott decision by the United States Supreme Court which divided North against South and slavery proponents against slavery opponents. Buchanan's problems were gargantuan. One way to divert the nation's attention from those apparently insurmountable troubles was to mount a campaign to replace the polygamous Brigham Young whom President Millard Fillmore, several years earlier had appointed governor. Clearly, Buchanan could replace him. "Sublimate the nation's concern for slavery to concern for polygamy." Brigham Young and his followers reacted with fury. Buchanan countered with an army of 2,500 soldiers from Fort Leavenworth, Kansas under command of Colonel Albert Sidney Johnston, who later was a Confederate General and Supreme Commander of the West when he surprised the Federal troops at Shiloh, another bloody battle. A bitter resentment welled in Amy's breast when she thought

of Shiloh, for that was the site of Brit's death. It was also
the battleground where General Albert Sidney Johnston had
received the wound which led to his death. A face saving
thrust and parry occurred between President Buchanan and
Brigham Young. After Young ordered the burning of Fort
Bridger and Fort Supply, the Federal troops spent the
winter on the eastern side of the Wasatch Mountains while
national sympathy swung to the Mormons. Buchanan, in
the grand style of national politics, compromised by forgiving
the Saints for their transgressions. Later, the Federal troops
marched through Salt Lake City on their way back to Kansas.
Cumming peacefully took office as governor.

"My goodness!" Amy thought raising her eyebrows,
"I thought I had troubles with marriage and men."

She started her trip on the following day through those
high rugged open mountains of the Wasatch. Now, however,
a transcontinental telegraph line and a heavily traveled freight
and stage line competed for space in the steep mountain
canyons with the track layers and graders.

Down the trail timbers now bridged the Weber River.
Swarms of track layers lifted rails into place. The ford
at the river was as treacherous as any she had ever seen.
"They call this Devil's Gate," shouted a buckskin clad
passenger, over the roar of the river.

"I can see why, by the looks of that river," she said.
"There is another landmark on the Sweetwater called
'Devil's Gate' isn't there?"

"That's right. Down near Independence Rock. Do you
know that place?"

"My father told me about it." Amy said. She looked out
the window at a myriad of colors that permeated the
landscape as the stage passed through Echo Canyon on its
last leg to Fort Bridger. They were earth colors, mostly.
Browns, grays, pale greens, and yellows; even gold. The
background of sandstone had been carved into huge domes

and spectacular formations, hinting of a red rock as its matrix.

Then finally the stage arrived at Fort Bridger and it was a disappointment. Fort Bridger was located on Black's Fork of the Green River. Amy had expected a high, log walled garrison with block houses guarding every corner and handsomely mounted cavalry troops practicing intricate parade ground maneuvers. Instead, right in the middle of four branches of Black's Creek was a long, low dirt roofed log house with a picket yard of poles set in the ground to protect the livestock. A dreary place, at best. Several half breed children peeked around the corners of the log structures. No cavalry was evident.

The stage rolled to a stop. "Come in, folks," said the proprietor. "Vittles on." A large cast iron kettle bubbled in the fireplace.

"Is Mr. Bridger here?"

"No, ma'am. He hasn't been here in a long time."

"Oh, I was so wanting to meet him."

"Last I heerd he was at Fort Lar'me," noted a teamster. "He's probably headed for Missouri. I don't think Old Gabe will be out here much anymore. His eyesight's getting bad."

CHAPTER THIRTEEN

STAGECOACH TO SOUTH PASS

She had spent a restless night in a hot, vermin-infested room and bed. Breakfast was chopped deer meat and coffee served without bread on a table swarming with flies. "What a filthy place! I hope South Pass City will be more appealing," she thought.

Amy spent very little time lingering at the table, instead she walked outside to get a breath of fresh air. On the stagecoach she saw, "Prescott Stage Line" neatly painted over the door. Four harnessed horses waited. They would reach South Pass in about eighteen hours, with a stop every twelve miles to change horses.

The driver, a tall, wiry man with a long handlebar moustache wore a large, wide-brimmed tan beaver felt hat pulled down tight to the top of his ears. Now finished with the harness, he watched Amy approach the team. "Mr. Prescott expected you about two weeks ago, Miss Stafford," he said.

"I was delayed in San Francisco."

"Have you had a good trip?"

"It has been enjoyable."

"My name's Harold James, ma'am. I'll be your driver from here to South Pass City. I think you'll like that town."

"I have heard so much about it, Mr. James. I can hardly wait to get there." She patted the neck of the nigh wheel horse, "Is Mr. Prescott in South Pass?"

"No, he's at the Platte crossing, ma'am." He smiled at her, "I sent a message this morning telling him that you're here at Fort Bridger and that you're just fine."

Shortly, the passengers boarded the coach and by noon they had journeyed up Black's Fork, crossed Ham's Fork and were on the west bank of the Green River.

This river, called the Seeds-kee-dee Agie by the Indians had a beautiful green hue and was full of beaver and trout. It was a deep, powerful stream that had taken the lives of many emigrants who tried to ford it. The Pony Express had used this same crossing for eighteen months until the Transcontinental Telegraph was completed in 1861. As soon as the telegraph lived, the Pony Express died.

Mr. James pulled the four-horse team to a stop alongside the unattended ferry. "I don't like it, Carl." James said to his helper. "Old Mose is usually here. Not like him to pass up $5.00."

"It's too dangerous, out here alone," admitted Carl. "I don't care how much money he makes." Carl looked up and down the river, "Don't see no sign of him."

At this moment, Amy interrupted them, "My goodness, Mr. James, this river looks deep." She paused and tried not to sound worried, "Is everything all right?"

The driver answered, "Yes, Miss Stafford, everything's just fine. We'll unhitch the team and swim the horses across sixty yards upstream. We'll then use the horses to help the current pull the ferry with the coach to the other side. We've lost more than one wagon at this ford. We have yet to lose a beautiful woman though. You hold on tight, hear?"

Her face was flushed with the excitement of danger. At Fort Bridger she had changed to a simple traveling suit, fashioned in San Francisco, with a short jacket, white laced blouse, buttoned to the neck, full skirt and high topped boots. Certainly she was more formally dressed than most travelers.

With a lurch, the force of the river threw the ferry into the current. Amy's heart seemed in her throat, "It's much swifter than I thought," she realized, while the ferry in a wide graceful arc, neared the eastern bank of the Seeds-kee-dee.

From Point of Rocks, the Prescott Line sent wagons to South Pass City over a seventy mile road bordering the western boundary of the Red Desert. While it was a shorter route than the course Amy traveled, it was much more dangerous. Being less traveled, it was a favorite target for road agents, outlaws and Sioux raiding parties.

The population of South Pass City had fluctuated greatly as rumors of new strikes drew the unlucky miners of South Pass City to better prospects. The closeness and high wages of the railroad caused a steady stream of workers coming and going on the roads. The miners knew they could make enough money working for the Union Pacific to grubstake their return to prospecting. The lure of possible high rewards in the gold fields drew them back to South Pass like a magnet. Some saw equal opportunity prospecting the pockets of the unwary traveling along the desolate stage roads.

Amy felt uneasy. She thought she saw horsemen on the horizon a half-mile to the south. "They're probably on their way to South Pass just like we are," she thought. Still, she couldn't keep from peeking out the window for a glimpse of the riders. Now two riders fell in behind the stage and kept about two hundred yards to the rear. Above, on the stage, Mr. James and his guard were uneasy.

"Three miles to Dry Sandy Stage Station," said the guard. He looked back at the road agents.

The stage had crossed the Little Sandy and was two miles beyond Sublette's Cutoff when two more mounted outlaws rode out of a deep sagebrush covered draw and faced the stage.

Mr. James' arm moved, "Yah!" he shouted as he cracked his whip over the ears of the lead horses. "We'll make a run for it!"

A barrage of shots slammed into the carriage, splintered wood fragments into the face of Amy Stafford who opened her leather shoulder bag and removed her Remington Double Deringer .41 rimfire short, tipped up the barrels to check the loads and closed the action just as a rider rode along side. She pointed the pistol and fired. The bandit slumped over the horn of his saddle, struggled to keep hold, lost his grip and fell to the ground. "Oh, my God!" Amy cried out, "I've killed him!"

On top of the coach, Carl's double barreled shotgun had an effect. The riders faded to the rear. By now they could see the stage station over the sagebrush. Station hands were outside with their rifles.

The exhausted, but highly excited stage team slammed to a halt in front of the log and rock structure.

"Heard the shootin'. Anybody hurt?" asked a rifleman.

"You all right, Miss?" asked another.

"I . . . I think so."

Mr. James, the driver, hit in the leg, bravely fought back tears of pain.

Amy went to his assistance. "I'll be all right, ma'am. It missed the bone." Mr. James grimaced.

Seeing that he was bleeding badly, she told the guard, "Carl, get my small trunk. I have some clean cloth there."

Carl unlashed the boot at the rear of the stage and retrieved the trunk. Amy dressed the wound as best she could, drew the ends of the bandage up tight, checked to see that the bleeding had slowed and turned to a station hand, "Is there a doctor in South Pass?"

"They've got a drug store there, ma'am. They carry medicines and dressings. No doctor though."

Outside, fresh horses waited for the twelve miles to South Pass and twenty to South Pass City. Carl took command, "Let's get Mr. James aboard. Easy now!" he exclaimed, "Put that trunk between the seats." The men lifted the injured man onto the seat, carefully supported his leg and after the others found seats closed the doors.

New horses and driver promised a record-setting pace. The Wind River Mountains loomed large to the north. Towering peaks were even taller sixty miles into the distance. On the southern end of this range the Continental Divide tapered to only 7400 feet after reaching its acme of over 13,000 feet some miles above. In 1842, while on his first explorer's expedition, John Charles Fremont, with Kit Carson and Charles Preuss in his party, had climbed a lesser peak in the Wind River Range and named it, "Fremont Peak", thinking incorrectly that this was Wind River's tallest. But, John Charles, the "Great Pathfinder", son-in-law of the senior Senator from Missouri, Thomas Hart Benton, was riding in ruts a foot deep made by mountain men during the previous thirty years. That he named the second highest peak to honor himself was understandable!

South Pass was not spectacular, just a gentle swell, and ruts from numerous wagons. The travelers followed Pacific Springs which irrigated a large meadow to a shining green in a land of browns, whites, grays and gold. Then by hugging the base of Pacific Butte, they crossed, almost unnoticed, the Continental Divide. There were no buildings there.

By 1824, Jedediah Smith and a party of mountain men including James Clyman, Bill Sublette and Tom Fitzpatrick had crossed South Pass from the east. The Crow Indian told them to follow the Popo Agie and then strike west through a gap to find the Seeds-kee-dee Agia, or Prairie Chicken River. The buffalo had traveled that route first, and next the Indians, and then probably others until Smith got word to General William H. Ashley, who widely publicised that route.

Just a mile over the summit the summer run-off from the southern Winds fed a clear swift stream called the Sweetwater. The stage stopped to water the horses. The passengers got out to stretch their legs. The June wind was cold. Now it was time to reach for a coat. A fine, cold mist threatened snow.

Carl instructed the passengers to find their seats. "Old Moses Harris and Bill Sublette walked from this point to St. Louis a good many years ago. Started in January. Took them just eight weeks. Now that was a pair," said the driver, as he jerked up his horses. "Get up, horse," he urged, and the stage creaked and rattled over the rocks of the river.

CHAPTER FOURTEEN

SOUTH PASS CITY

From the right side of the stage Amy saw open, rolling foothills, treeless and harsh, the beginning of the southern Wind River Mountains.

"South Pass City!" shouted the driver.

Amy looked out the window and saw no town, just the bare hills. She was disappointed. "You can't see it from here," said Mr. James who had awakened from a nap. "We'll have to top that hill," he pointed.

At the top of the hill, they were a half mile from town on a wind-swept mountain with the sun to the back of the stage. Amy held her hat tightly and stuck her head out the window. "What a quaint little town," she thought. It was down in a deep canyon that housed over fifty buildings. Willows covered the upper valley for one hundred yards on the south side of the creek. At least a hundred head of horses and mules were in the corral bordering Willow Creek and enclosed by a pole fence. A huge haystack stood against the Black Horse Livery that was the largest complex of buildings in town. From her vantage on the stage road and looking down on the town, she could see every building in the valley. Horses stood along the rails in front of the several hotels, saloons and stores. "That wagon, Mr. James, where is it coming from?"

"That's the Carissa Mine above the town, there on the side of the hill," he pointed. "It's one of their ore wagons."

Running right through the little town was Willow Creek with its banks covered by thick, low willows, the areas only trees. South of the creek was a stamp mill. "What's that thing, Mr. James?"

"That's a rock crushing device." As they neared the crusher, he told her the nature of its construction and the manner of its use. Constructed of hewn timbers which supported ten iron bars affixed to a drive shaft, turned by a water-powered wheel fastened to its end, the blacksmith had forged heavy round iron cylinders to the end of each bar. The cam construction of the drive shaft produced a reciprocating motion to the bars' heavy cylinder.

"It looks rather complicated," she stated, a puzzled expression on her face.

"There's nothing to it, really. See that hopper at the bottom? The miners dump rock into the thing, and the cylinders stamp the stuff into powder. It'll make sense after you see one in operation."

Now they passed the Black Horse Livery; its main stable was a building twenty-five feet wide and forty feet long built in three log sections. It had a lean-to shed on the west side and a heavy plank floor. Butted against the stage road were three low log buildings with a high, but small corral. Its pole fence was about seven feet high. These buildings quartered a blacksmith and harness shop and had enough room inside to repair wagons. One large storage area held sacks of grain, mostly oats and corn.

A freight wagon parked outside the livery was empty.

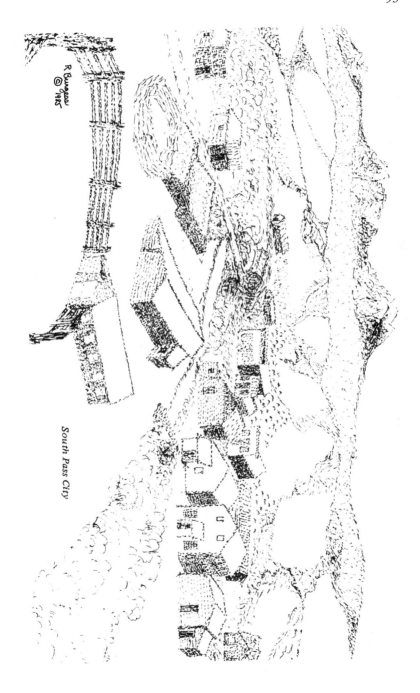

South Pass City

R Burgess
© 1985

Mr. James told Amy that one of these wagons could haul three tons of hay and that the common practice was to haul hay from the Sweetwater or from End of Track. "Three wagons are hooked together and pulled by a jerkline of twelve to eighteen mules," he said.

The Black Horse Livery was comfortable quarters for Prescott's horses and mules. A footbridge led from the livery across the creek and into the back of the Willow Bend Saloon. Next door was the Exchange Bank and Assay Office; on the other side the Prescott Hotel and Stage Station, a two-story frame building with a balcony porch supported by large, log pillars. Four other hotels catered to the miners' needs. A dozen saloons quenched the thrist of lonely men seeking the comfort of whiskey and women. These charmers knew how to mine for gold. Across the street was a long low general store and next to it Jackson's Drug Store.

The drug store would be patronized just as soon as Carl could get his partner into the Prescott Hotel. "Give me a hand, boys," he said to the men on the porch. "Mr. James has been shot!"

Amy stepped out of the stagecoach onto the street assisted by a passenger and met by the silent, admiring stares of the many miners in the crowd. Evidence of gold mining was everywhere. The district had hundreds of mines. Some were just placers, others coyote holes, holes simply dug back into a hill for three or four feet and down for six feet, and shored with timbers. But there were four major mines like the Carissa within six miles of South Pass City like the one over in Atlantic Gulch. Sluice boxes and rockers were a common sight. Lonely prospectors with their mules carrying their ever needful pick, shovel, gold pan and rifle scoured the hills for a precious outcrop of color. Most hadn't found it.

Iron pyrite was everywhere and the miners' hands were always covered with its golden sheen. At the Carissa mine, from which most of the Sweetwater gold was coming, stood a headframe, surrounded by a series of buildings. From one of those buildings a covered track carried ore cars about a hundred yards to the mill which consisted of four buildings arranged like the steps of a stairway down the side of the hill toward the town. The new sawmill's first boards had gone into the construction of the headframe, mine buildings and mill. It was in those buildings that the quartz was crushed, washed and amalgamated with mercury to glean the finest particle of flour gold for the sack.

While Amy stood in the crowd, a rather attractive woman greeted her obsequiously, "Amy, darling! Howard has told me how devine you are!"

"I doubt if that is the word, Miss . . . Miss?"

"Call me Lil. Oh, how rude of me. Lillian Montgomery. I run this business for Howard."

"Oh, I see."

"Won't you come in. I have a room ready for you. Howard asked me to take good care of you."

It didn't take Amy long to see to the placement of her trunks. Stacked along one wall and alongside the bed, they almost took up all the room in the small second floor quarters. A stand along one wall held a pitcher of water and a large basin with a wall mirror above it. She stood before the mirror; dust stains smudged her jacket and streaked her face. She removed her jacket, poured the basin half-full of water and washed her face, patting it dry with a towel. "My, that feels much better!" she said to herself. Sorting through her trunk, she removed a floor length gown of silk with appliqued pink and yellow primroses splashed across the lower third of the dress. The bodice, modestly cut, was of narrow, horizontal strips of taffeta, pink and yellow. Pleased with her selection, she finished dressing for dinner.

"What a lovely dress," Lillian said. "Dinner is ready. Won't you come in and sit down?"

"Thank you, Miss Montgomery." She walked into a

large building connected to the hotel which housed the
kitchen and dining hall. This first meal of baked goods fresh
each day from their own ovens and fresh meat from the
town's butcher shop delighted Amy. "I haven't had a meal
like this since I left Sacramento!"

"Howard's, . . . Mr. Prescott's wagons haul supplies up here
from End of Track at least once daily."

"Miss   Montgomery,   how   long   have   you   known
Mr. Prescott?"

"Howard and I have been friends and business partners
for years, dear. How long have you known him?"

"Not very long, I'm afraid."

"Well, you should feel lucky to have hooked a fellow
like Howard. He's a wealthy man. He tries to hide it, but
everyone knows he hauls gold out of here on every trip."

"I do declare, Miss Lillian, don't they get held up?"

"Once in a while, honey, but he can afford it!"

The meal finished, Lillian showed Amy about the hotel.
Lillian's room was pleasant. It was actually two rooms with
the wall removed between them and a stove installed at one
end. A chest of drawers and a wash stand and large trunk
added to the comfort of the room with its large double bed.

Alone, Amy went to her room, retrieved her shoulder bag,
locked the door and walked down the stairs to the dark
street. The Black Horse Saloon was across the road from the
livery. It was busy night and day. Built of logs and two
stories high, its stairway on the outside led to small rooms
for the girls above. Downstairs, the dark interior was lighted
by shaded coal oil lamps suspended from the ceiling. Even
in the dimness Amy's radiant beauty brought a hush to the
din of the miners' revelry.

"Now looky here!" squealed a tipsy miner as he pinched
Amy's bottom. Guffaws coursed through the crowd. Quiet
returned quickly after Amy turned to the bartender and
asked softly, "Do you know Harry Montagu?"

"Lots of 'Harrys' in this camp, Miss. I don't know any 'Montagus'." Loudly, the bartender shouted above the racket, "Harry Montagu!"

From a dark corner an average sized, thin man said in a loud, unrestrained voice, "Amy! Amy! Is that you? I've been looking for you for two weeks! I didn't think you were coming. My gosh, it's good to see you. Here," he said, holding her at arms' length; "let me look at you."

"Give her a kiss, Harry!" shouted a miner.

Harry tried to ignore the crowd but kissed Amy hungrily on the mouth. The crowd roared its approval.

"Bartender, send a bottle of wine over to my table." He took Amy by the arm, escorted her across the room and held her chair for her. "Tell me about your trip," he said excitedly, sitting down beside her. "You said the first week of June. I've been in this hole for two weeks!"

"Harry, darling, I've come thousands of miles. Two little weeks shouldn't mean much," she pouted. "How is Montana?" Amy asked.

"Virginia City, Montana is just like this place only bigger. More money, more mines, more people." He stopped and thought a minute. "More people get killed up there; this town is kind of tame by contrast. I'll show you the jail tomorrow. It's right in back of this saloon. These folks don't have a sheriff here, just vigilante justice. One of these miners spends the night in that jail, he sobers up real quick. That log jailhouse has four tiny rooms with doors about four feet high. A prisoner in one of those cells feels like a rat."

"Haven't you found anything to do here?"

"Well, that Lil likes to talk."

"You stay away from her!"

"She's just lonely," he suggested.

"Lonely my foot. With all these men?"

"Let's go to my cabin where we won't be overheard," he said.

CHAPTER FIFTEEN

A POKE OF GOLD

After Amy left his cabin to return to the hotel, Harry walked across the street to the Willow Bend Saloon. He had much to do in the next two days. "This place is jumping tonight," he thought, opening the batwing doors of the noisy saloon. The roulette table, crowded with miners and a few women dressed in low cut, black lace gowns, clattered with the sound of the ball falling into the pocket. The bar, full from end to end and in some places two deep offered no sanctuary for a thirsty traveler. All the gaming tables were occupied, so he walked out the back door and crossed Willow Creek over the foot bridge and around the livery to the Black Horse Saloon across the street.

"Look who's here," said the miner. "Thought you'd be out for the night," he laughed.

"Couldn't handle that little woman?" he teased.

"Send her over here, Harry; we'll take care of her!" sang another.

"I'd rather hire you than fight you, boys. What say we talk over a drink? Bartender! Bring us a bottle."

"We don't mean nothin', Harry. You know that. Hell, she's a looker, that's all."

The miner and his friend joined Harry at a table. Harry poured each a shot glass full of whiskey.

"I need a wagon and a team," said Harry, softly.

"Hell, that's easy," said one miner loudly. "Old Jenkins will fix you up in the morning."

"I need you two to help me take a load of water about thirty miles south of here."

"Down to the Sandy?" asked the miner.

"No, east of there."

"Out in the desert?"

"That's right," said Harry. "Out in the desert."

"But there's nothing out there."

"Look, I'll pay you twice your wages. No, I'll do even better than that. One hundred dollars apiece for two days' work."

"When do we leave?" asked the friend.

"Tomorrow morning," said Harry, firmly. "Meet me at the livery at daybreak."

The following morning five empty fifty-gallon barrels were in a wagon and two hundred pounds of grain securely loaded when the two arrived.

"Two horses should be enough for this light load," said Harry. "We'll tie our ponies behind for the trip back."

The freight wagon bounced up the long hill past the mine to the Point of Rocks stage road between Rock Creek and Willow Creek. Moving easily down a long gentle hill, its passengers rolled with the undulations of the wagon as the iron ringed oak wheels crossed Willow Creek just five miles above the Sweetwater. They would cross that stream in about an hour.

"What are you doing out in the desert?" asked the miner.

"Just some business," Harry replied, quietly.

"You haven't found color out there have you?" questioned the miner's friend with a knowing wink toward his partner.

"No," laughed Harry.

The treeless banks of the Sweetwater supported tall sagebrush and willows which grew close to the river's edge, but parched sagebrush twenty yards from the stream fought a tenuous battle with the persistent wind. Harry flicked the reins over the backs of the horses, driving them into the middle of the stream. They threw one barrel over the side and into the river. They filled the barrels, replaced the lids and lifted them back onto the wagon.

"Damn dry country out there," said the miner with a nod to the south.

"Last water we'll see for the next thirty miles," said Harry. "Let's be on our way."

They had skirted Oregon Buttes on its east side as they continued south into the desert. By midafternoon the wagon turned north of the Pinnacles and deeper into the desert. A very sparse cover of grass mixed with alkali and sand with a few scrawny sagebrush clumps dotted the desert floor.

Harry drove the wagon into a long shallow draw that just barely hid the side boards and barrel tops. "I want this wagon out of sight!" he said, tossing a shovel to each man. "A foot and a half. That should be deep enough. Lean into it and let's get out of here!"

The hole finished, Harry led the horses forward until the wagon dropped into the trenches. "Unhitch the team and leave the harness in the wagon."

"Sure seems strange to me," said the miner.

"What's that?" asked Harry.

"Why you'd bring that water out here. Ain't nothing out here."

Harry thought a moment, "How'd you boys like to make some real money?"

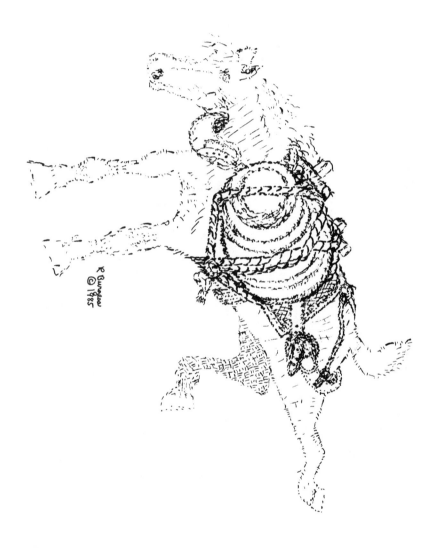

Both men grinned, "We're interested," one of the miners said.

After saddling their horses, they started north to the Sweetwater and town, leading the two draft horses. "What's the job, Harry?" said the miner.

"I'll tell you all about it back in town."

Later that evening, after dark, they passed the campfires of an emigrant wagon train but stayed east of them. If their progress was unhindered, the emigrant party would pass through Pacific Springs Station, just eight miles ahead, the next night and probably make camp there.

A three-quarter moon reflected off the river of the Sweetwater while the three men stopped to fill their canteens and water the horses. Daylight broke while Harry and the pair of riders entered South Pass City just as Amy dressed for breakfast.

She had awakened early, washed her hair and rolled it tightly in a bun at the back of her head. Amy entered the dining room where two tables, seating six people each, had been occupied by many hungry miners during the past two hours. The cook and his helpers had used a large table in the kitchen for preparing a hardy breakfast of buffalo and elk steaks, and chops fried in bacon grease; the drippings made a thick gravy. Hot biscuits, baked in the oven of the wood stove, and a large crock of honey satisfied the appetites of daily patrons.

None of the girls were up yet, so Amy received the undivided attention of the miners as she sat down to breakfast. She wore a beaver hat with fur trim and a tall crown creased down the middle. The dark brown beaver matched the color of her light-weight vest which partially covered a brilliantly white silk blouse. A tan riding skirt cut to the top of her tan riding boots completed her dress. Lillian, dressed plainly, came out of the kitchen with a cup of coffee and sat down beside her.

"There isn't much to do here, Miss Stafford, but I'll be happy to show you around our little town."

"Thank you, Lillian. I am eager to see the mine."

"I'm afraid there isn't much to see. It's just a dirty, noisy place with a lot of rock being crushed."

"Do you think I'll be able to see the gold?" asked Amy.

"Sure. We'll watch them put it in canvas bags if you'd like.

An hour after breakfast a light buckboard rolled to a stop in front of the hotel where the waiting women boarded it for the trip up the hill to the mine where the superintendent greeted them.

"Miss Stafford, this is where we crush the rock!" he shouted over the noise of the four stamp mills.

"There is a lot more rock than I thought," she said, "and I don't see any gold."

"We get just about enough gold out of one ton of rock to make one twenty dollar gold piece," he explained. "Come with me, I'll show you the final product."

The door closed behind them, shutting out the noise of the mill and the guide said, "Watch your step, ladies; this stairway is rather steep."

"This is exciting," Amy said, laughingly. "I have never been in a gold mine before."

They approached a heavy locked door and paused while the superintendent rapped for entry. A small viewing panel slid open and a face appeared. Presently, the heavy door swung open, and the trio entered.

"Oh, my goodness, it's beautiful!" said Amy, looking around the long, heavily-guarded shed where gold was being weighed, and sacked.

"Most of what you see will assay twelve dollars to the ounce," said the guide.

"I thought I handled gold in my business, but I have never

seen anything like this," marveled Amy, "How much is all this worth?"

"What you can see;" he stated, "about half a million."

Lillian turned to Amy, "Now, that would keep a girl in jewels and furs, wouldn't it?" she smiled.

Amy thanked the superintendent for his hospitality. "I didn't know what to expect. Your tour of the mine was most educational. Thank you, sir."

"My pleasure, Miss. Please accept this, with our best wishes." He handed her a small leather sack with a rawhide drawstring, which contained a tiny sample of gold dust.

Amy beamed her thanks. "Oh, how exciting. Again, I thank you!"

As they walked down the hill toward the buckboard, Lillian said, "Watch that old geezer. He spends several ounces of dust every night on the girls at the Black Horse."

With a chuckle, Amy replied, "At least it sounds like he knows how to take his mind off all that gold."

All afternoon Amy walked about the town, visited with storeowners, shopped for items for the trip to End of Track and enjoyed the friendliness of the townspeople. A warm, soft breeze drifted up from the plain of the Sweetwater as the dinner hour neared.

That evening, after their meal of fried trout, that the cook had caught in willow basket traps, Harry took Amy to the Black Horse for entertainment at the gaming tables.

"You're not really going to marry this Prescott fellow are, you, Amy?"

She looked at him with a smile and didn't answer.

"Come with me to Virginia City. There is excitement there. Real money. You and I could start a gambling parlor and saloon. We could make a fortune!"

"I left that in New Orleans, Harry."

"Well, what are you looking for?"

"I have come to marry Howard."

"But you're not going to marry him. You could have married him in New Orleans!"

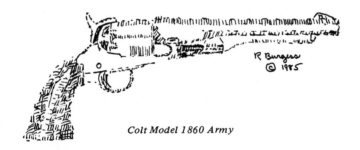

Colt Model 1860 Army

CHAPTER SIXTEEN

PRAIRIE WOLF

Jedediah awakened to the faint bark of a prairie wolf. It was barely light enough to see, and the sound of the river and the slight rustling of the pine boughs by the wind muffled the wolf's cry. He lay in his warm blankets for a few minutes and then propped himself up on one elbow. He cocked his ear toward his horses, heard another yelping, short bark which made him quickly throw back his blanket, and put on his pistol belt. He then looked at the caps in his shotgun and revolver. He pulled on his boots; his trousers would have to wait. He felt his heart race as he slowly and quietly levered a round into the chamber of his Henry, and then he set it aside. He worked his way around the rock ledge and stared into the darkness. He could make out one horse but couldn't see his other. He could see the dim outline of a wolf inching its way to his picketed horse. He cocked the hammers of his shotgun and fired. Over his right shoulder from the top of the outcrop, a dark figure leaped headfirst toward him as Jed whirled and fired. The buckshot caught the Indian plumb center. A yipping battle cry came from three mounted warriors as they led Jed's pack-horse over the ridge. "God damit," he hissed, through his teeth, "slept too long this morning."

"Sioux," he noted, as he turned over the wolf-skin covered Indian. "Paid dearly for one horse," he said, aloud.

Now he knew that the pack animals' loads would have to be pared down and carried on his mount. He wouldn't be able to take much of it with him. He fed his horse an extra ration of grain and emptied the rest on the ground, "The mice will have full bellies tonight," he thought.

Sorting through his panniers, he laid out the supplies he would take. "Hell, everything I own is right here. But Howie will probably have all of this stuff, too." Still, he kept his buckshot and a hundred rounds of each of his cartridges. And his coffee pot.

"Going to be a long day. No need of throwing away this slab of bacon," he thought, as he sliced all of it into the skillet. His coffee was already boiling by the time he saddled his horse.

He rolled his blanket with the ammunition inside and tied it across the saddle horn, cavalry style. His saddle bags were full, and his heavy wool coat, rolled to hold his extra shirt, he tied behind the cantle. He favored buckskins for his mountain clothing and that was what he was wearing now. His hat was of beaver with a short visor. He didn't care for moccasins, but rather preferred heavy boots worn inside his buckskin breeches.

He slipped the bit of the bridle into the horse's mouth, buckled the strap of the headstall, wrapped the rein around a limb and turned to the fire to kick the ashes cold. With one last look about the campsite he mounted his horse and urged it down the river-bank.

First light broke over Platte Ridge as his horse walked quickly down the game trail. When he had first come to these

mountains about fifteen years before, the lack of horses
played an important part in a fight that took place to the
west just over his left shoulder. That there had been one of
the worst winters he ever remembered; it killed almost every
horse in this part of the mountains and plains. For resupply,
the trappers drove up horses from Mexico and California.
A fierce contest with the Indians for these mounts took
place. Many lives were lost near a peak that had since been
known as Battle Mountain.

"Tough country without horses," he thought. "Tough
country with them," he chuckled. "Damn, I love it!"

On down the river, at the warm springs a small village of
Sioux stood along the bank. Women and children gathered
choke-cherries. He gave them a wide berth by heading
straight west for two miles and then north nine miles to
Platte Crossing on the Overland Trail. This put him just
fifteen miles from End of Track.

When he arrived at the Platte Crossing the Station Master
and his helpers were shoeing horses. The big man in the
leather apron hardly looked up. "Step down, mister. 'Spect
you could use some grub."

"Much obliged," said Jedediah.

"Injuns been raising hell along this line, mister. I'd watch
my backtrail."

"Ran into some this morning. Stole my pack-horse. Two
of them won't steal anymore."

"Where you headed?"

"End of Track."

"We've been hearing reports about that hellhole."

"Have you heard of Howard Prescott?"

"Prescott? Yea, he's freightin' out of there and up on the
Sweetwater. Hell of a hand, I hear. Got held up three or four
days ago. Injuns or road agents, I'm not sure."

Jedediah looked toward the corral. "Good horses," he
motioned. "How long you lived here?"

"Little over two years."

"Much traffic on this road?"

"Not anymore. Not since Fort Sanders. Come on in the cabin. Coffee's hot."

Jedediah tied his horse to a pole in the corral fence and loosened the cinch on the saddle.

"Martin, put a nose-bag on the man's horse and give him some corn."

The young, skinny helper laid his hammer on a stump and replied, "Yes sir, Mr. Miller."

"My name's Jacob Miller," said the big man, offering his hand.

"Jedediah Caldwell, Mr. Miller." The two men walked into the cabin with its dirt floor and rough-sawed plank table. The aroma of coffee and harness leather filled the air. Miller poured two tin cups full of coffee and set them on the table. He commenced to slice bacon into a heavy skillet. "It was two years ago," he began. "Before the railroad. Fort Sanders was established over on the Laramie River. Of course, there weren't a town then. Just the army on Soldier Creek. Called it Fort John Buford at first. That was in '66. I mustered out of the cavalry the same year." Into a second skillet he sliced thin slivers of potato.

"Did you help build Fort Sanders?" asked Jedediah.

"No. I was stationed at Fort Halleck. 11th Ohio. I was there from start to finish. 1862 until July 4, 1866. It was on the north end of Elk Mountain. The Colonel sent us pony soldiers all up and down this Overland Trail. Clear from Camp Collins down in Colorado Territory on west to Fort Bridger. Old Doc Finfrock, at Fort Halleck, had his work cut out for him. If it weren't for gunshot and arrow wounds, it was freezing to death or frost-bite!"

"Why did they move the stage from the Oregon Trail south here to the Overland Trail?" asked Jedediah.

"Oregon Trail," Jacob said incredulously. "Sublette's Trail!

What did you say your name was? Jedediah, weren't it?" He
didn't stop to let Jed speak, but continued, warming to his
subject. "Jedediah's Trail, after your namesake, Jedediah
Smith. The greatest explorer ever to come west!" He glared
at Jedediah.

"Well, Jacob, I have to agree with you. There were a lot
of good men who ran that trail. Walked it, too. James
Clyman, Tom Fitzpatrick, and Moses Harris."

"Yeah, not to mention 'Old Gabe', Jim Bridger!" said Jacob.

Jedediah didn't have the heart to tell him that he was
named after his father, Jedediah Caldwell, Sr., but said,
"You still haven't told me why they moved the trail south."

"Injuns. Sioux mostly. 'Course it weren't no better down
here. Worse stretch was between Fort Halleck just to the
east of us, and right here at the Platte Crossing and on west
to Bridger's Pass. Huh! You talk about names. Bridger was
an old man before he found his pass. Should be called
'Ashley's Pass'!"

Jedediah didn't say anything because he knew the story
was coming. He liked this big man with the rough hands.

"William Ashley took this very trail up from Colorado.
Right through where this cabin stands and on through what's
called 'Bridger's Pass'. That was in 1825, Fitzpatrick and
Clyman were with him. They were taking a pack-train of
goods to the first Rendezvous on Henry's Fork of the Green.
Fitzpatrick and Clyman walked back to St. Louis from the
head of the Sweetwater. You know how far that is?"

"Yes, sir. I've been up and down that trail myself. I
was born in St. Louis."

"Then you know it ought not be called the Oregon Trail!"

Jedediah smiled and finished his potatoes and bacon.
"Did you ever meet Lieutenant Collins, Jacob?"

"Colonel William Collins and his son, Lieutenant Caspar
Collins were at Fort Halleck from time to time. The boy
was killed at Platte Bridge in '65. Called that place Fort

Caspar after that. This is great country, Jedediah, but that railroad is going to ruin it. They'll be bringing plows in here next thing!"

"You and I won't live to see that day, Jacob."

"Huh. Damn glad of that!"

Jed cut a thick slice of bread with his sheath knife, replaced the knife and helped himself to the last of the potatoes and bacon. After finishing his second cup of coffee, he said, "I thank you for the fixin's. I'd best be getting along."

"You're welcome. You have a safe journey."

Ahead the country opened into a wide plain as flat as a tabletop. He could see Elk Mountain and Rattlesnake Pass twenty miles to the east. Straight north a low cedar ridge acted as a bulwark against which the Platte River had nibbled away at the red outcrop.

"Those scrub trees aren't makin' much of a living on that slope," he thought, as he kicked his horse to a canter.

By evening a thick cloud of reddish dust layered along the river and up against the low ridge partially hiding the numerous campfires all up and down the stream. Rows of army tents pitched along the broken ground in an attempt to simulate military order shone red in the evening sun. Available space for a camp was quite limited. In a narrow strip along the river, willows had taken command and cottonwood trees survived only a few yards from its bank. There were wild rose bushes, but otherwise the ground was barren. It looked as if a huge buffalo herd had pulverized every square inch. The red dust was ankle deep and stifling, even without a wind.

A crew working around the clock bridged the river. They used oil torches for lighting. Mules on each side pulled a ferry across the river, and a raft of logs stretched up the river as far as the eye could see.

A wye in the tracks, built a half mile from the river, allowed for off loading of supplies, and for the past ten days

hundreds of track followers had erected a tent city on a
narrow flat of sagebrush south of the cavalry garrison. It
had grown to fifteen hundred men and about a dozen women.
Brownsville they called it and named after an assistant
engineer of construction who had been gut shot in the Red
Desert west of there and had died after being carried fifteen
miles across the sagebrush flats to LaClede Station on the
Overland Trail. Not much of an epitaph. These track
followers, this collection of scum and trash, had run ahead
of the vigilantes' rope and out of the lawless cities along
the track.

A huge tent, erected on a wooden deck with a large neatly
lettered sign clear across the twenty-five foot front read,
"Brent and Co., Wines and Liquors." Inside, a richly carved
bar and back bar with large mirrors dominated the west
wall. Tables for gambling jammed its fifty foot length. At
least a half-dozen armed men with double barreled shotguns
sat on high stools watching every move. Smaller tents with
wooden false fronts simply marked, "Saloon" filled any
empty spot along the dusty street.

There had already been a half-dozen killings in the first
few days of life in this hole of wickedness. The law was at
the bottom of sunrise and that was where this bunch of
ruffians wanted it, miles to the east.

Jedediah walked his horse through the narrow streets,
saw his friend standing between two long stacks of railroad
ties with a leather case in his hand.

Now Howard saw Jedediah coming toward him. "Hello,
Howie! How the hell are you?" asked Jedediah.

CHAPTER SEVENTEEN

THE PLAN

Howard carried a long leather case full of maps of the region. A big man, six feet two inches, two hundred twenty pounds with brown eyes and short, straight brown hair, he wore a wide brimmed black felt hat with a tall crown. A black string tie at the collar of his white shirt contrasted with the fringed leather jacket he wore which covered his Colt 1860 Army .44 percussion revolver. Knee length black leather boots, freshly polished that morning and worn outside his black trousers, were now covered with thick reddish dust. A wide grin spread across his face. He walked through the staging area of construction supplies to greet his friend, "Jedediah, it has been a long time."

"That it has, Howie; that it has."

"Come to my tent. The others are waiting."

Prescott had erected two wall tents end to end with bunks for the men. Inside, Jimmy Robineaux and Charles Richfield waited.

"Just like old times," said Charles. "Good to see you, Jed," he extended his hand.

"Long trip up from Denver," said Jimmy. "Thought I was going to have to go get you," he added with a smile.

"Got slowed down this morning. Had to repack my goods. Sioux made off with my pack-horse."

"What's up, Howie?" asked Jed.

"$200,000.00 dollars in gold dust."

"Whew," whistled Jed. "How'd it happen?"

"The gold isn't all they got. They abducted my fiancée, Amy Stafford. On my own stage line! I should have been with her. I could just as easily have met her in San Francisco."

"It could have happened anywhere, Howard," explained Jimmy.

"I guess you're right," admitted Howard.

Pinning his map to the end of the tent, he discussed the general lay of the land. "You've all been through some of this. Jimmy has covered all of it. The stage left South Pass City five days ago. There were four passengers including Amy. There was one driver and a guard. Both were heavily armed. Traveling with them was one of my freight wagons. Normally I would have had two or three freight wagons hooked together, but 10 mules were pulling just one large wagon. It had one skinner and his helper. The gold was in forty pound sacks. There were twenty-four of them weighing about a thousand pounds. We hid these sacks among barrels of flour. We've always done it this way, but this is the largest haul we've tried to move."

"Where did they get bushwhacked?" inquired Jedediah.

"About five miles down the river on the west bank. They had a four-man infantry escort on the freight wagon that they had picked up at Sweetwater Station."

"Then what happened?" asked Chuck.

"After they left Sweetwater Station, they continued on down the river thirty miles to Split Rock." He punched the map. "They changed horses and drivers there. The army escort stayed with them. They turned south for ten miles and entered Whiskey Gap. It's about forty miles from there to where they were attacked." Howard traced the route across the map.

"Any idea who did it?" offered Jim.

"A deserter from this garrison. A lieutenant named Sampson and a corporal. About twelve of them all told as near as I can make out. They recruited some of this riff-raff. It wasn't hard to gather a bunch of hard cases from this filth."

"Many killed?" asked Jed.

"More than I had feared. That lieutenant stole a Mountain Gatling Gun from the quartermaster tent. Had it loaded on three mules. It hadn't even been uncrated. The thing is awesome. Fires a .58 caliber rimfire with a 565 grain bullet as fast as you turn the handle. Got about ten barrels on it, I think. They caught the wagons in a narrow gorge. The army boys put up a good fight, but they didn't have a chance. That big slug just about destroyed the freight wagon. I counted eight bodies plus one of the attackers when we buried them."

"Has the cavalry gone after them?" continued Jed.

"What they could spare. About ten men. They've got one infantry company and one cavalry company here. The infantry company stays with the train, and the cavalry has 8,000 square miles to patrol. The cavalry detail returned yesterday. They lost them in the desert."

Jimmy stood, taking the willow pointer from Howard and explained, "They've got a three-day headstart. They are heavily-armed and well-mounted. They could go straight north through the Seminoe Gap," he traced on the map, "or back through Whiskey Gap, the way the wagons came. If they edged along Green Mountain, they would cut through Crook's Gap. They could cross the divide above Bastard Butte; there are several small lakes up there," he thumped

on the map. "The next crossing would be this side of
Oregon Buttes."

"How about south?" asked Charles.

"Suicide. No water." said Jimmy.

"Then that's probably what they'll do," suggested Charles.
"They know the whole damn army will be following them.
That's what I'd do."

"Did they take the wagon with them?" wondered Jed.

"No. There was a large number of horses and mules
though. They would need five or six mules just for the gold
if they wanted to travel fast."

"They might hole up for a few days. There's good water
on Seminoe Mountain. It's closest too," said Jim.

"The army lost them on a northerly course," countered
Howie. "I doubt that they'd double back."

"Did the cavalry patrol on to the Sweetwater?"
inquired Charles.

"Yes," answered Howie, "They didn't cross their tracks.

"Then they have to be out here," stated Jedediah, pointing
to the area of the Red Desert.

"That's what I think," agreed Charles.

"Looks like it," nodded Jim.

"Then it's a consensus?" frowned Howie.

They all nodded.

"Very well. Then I suggest we strike due west forty miles
and then turn north to cut their tracks. Comments?"

"We'll need water," said Jim. "Fifteen miles straight west
is Rawlins Springs. I suggest we take mules with barrels.
We can fill them there. As each load is used up, cut the
mule loose, he'll find water. Probably return right back here
to the Platte.

"Good idea," said Howie. "I've got a whole corral full
of mules. We'll pack what we need."

"Supplies?" inquired Jed. "I'm low on rifle ammunition."

"That's what I've been busy doing these past three days,"

Howie said. "I've got panniers full of supplies with the ammunition dispersed throughout the bunch in case we lose some animals. Two mules will carry six hundred pounds of grain. Their load will lighten fast. We'll grain just those animals that we intend to see through to the end. We'll grain our animals twice a day for the first three days. That will require just under a hundred pounds of oats per day. Any lame stock we've got we'll turn loose. I figure we'll be in the saddle about sixteen hours a day and these critters won't have much time to forage," said Howie. He had learned from Joe Walker, who had led a party across the California desert in 1833, that the way to engage in an expedition of this kind was to be well mounted and each man leading three pack horses or mules.

"Damn Sioux going to have a field day gathering all that loose stock," laughed Charles.

"What say we have steak and whiskey? Might even find a poker game among all these high rollers," grinned Howard.

"By damn this place is hell for noise," said Jimmy, as they walked four abreast between the tents toward the gambling halls.

Jimmy noted the two streets, trampled out of the sagebrush, ankle deep in choking red powder. A tiny whirlwind of dust raced across the street and slammed into a dirty canvas tarp rigged as a lean-to. During the first hours of construction of this tent city order was attempted, but then a haphazard arrangement of tents, with their guy ropes overlapping, created hazards to horses and pedestrians alike. From an hour after sundown on, this tent town wouldn't slow down until about four in the morning.

"This place ought to have a steak," said Howie, pointing to a tent with a painted sign on the canvas wall that simply said, "EATS". Two twelve by fourteen foot tents stood end to end and had a plank floor in place. Sawdust covered the decking to muffle the sound of scraping feet.

"What will it be, boys?" asked a big man with a flour sack apron around his waist.

"The biggest steak you've got, for each of us," said Howie, "And a bottle of whiskey."

"Look at that big cook stove he's got in the back and all those utensils. Hell, just like a hotel!"

"About everything you see was hauled by the railcars. One day they will put the freight wagon out of business." Howard poured a round of whiskey, and then said, "I'm proud to have you boys with me. Here's to your health."

"And," Charles said, "to as fine a leader as ever sat a horse!"

"How did you get all this started, Howard? Last time I saw you, you were just getting out of the cavalry," said Jedediah.

"I started with two thousand dollars. Every dime I made I put into mules and wagons. It just kept growing."

Meanwhile, the cook busily prepared their meal while they had their second round of whiskey.

The cook brought a kettle of beans and a loaf of freshly baked bread and mashed potatoes. "Man, look at those steaks," said Charles.

Jimmy cut into his steak and took a bite. "How far does your line run, Howie?" asked Jimmy.

"End of Track to South Pass City. Then to Fort Bridger to the west and Fort Laramie to the east and to Cheyenne. We get down the Overland Trail some. I've pulled back from the Indian Country north of the Platte. We haul everything. And God knows, the people need it."

"Running that gold is kind of dangerous, isn't it?" asked Charles.

"It wasn't, up until now. It's a risky business even without the gold."

"What say we have a round of five card stud and then turn in?" offered Howie.

CHAPTER EIGHTEEN

DOWN THE SWEETWATER

Through the small window of her room Amy saw the stagecoach where six horses, driven by twos and hitched in place, patiently waited the day's run. They would change horses at St. Mary's Station, but the same driver would continue for the entire journey.

After breakfast, with her trunks stowed safely aboard the coach, Amy walked to the door of the stagecoach where she was met and assisted to her seat by Harry Montagu who sat beside her for the trip to End of Track. "How are you this morning, Harry?"

"I don't feel like riding in a stage today, but with you along it will be a pleasure," he grinned.

Ten mules, hitched to a large freight wagon, stood calmly while men stacked boxes and barrels to the top of the high sideboards. The workers lashed a heavy tarpaulin over the top with several long rawhide ropes.

"Tell Mr. Prescott hello for me," said Lillian, as she waved goodbye to Amy.

"I shall do that, Lillian. We will be coming back through here, I'm sure," said Amy.

The wagon boss of the freight wagon uncoiled his bull whip and with an expertly aimed "crack" yelled, "Get up, mules!" as the line heaved into their traces. The skinner skillfully guided them over the bridge.

"It is amazing how that long line of mules can be made to turn and pivot at precisely the point where the teamster wants," she thought. His helper rode the nigh wheel mule for extra control while they worked their way over the bridge and through the narrow street between the buildings.

Up the hill past the Carissa Mine they turned east down Rock Creek to the Sweetwater. In two hours they were following the deep ruts of the Oregon Trail, but in the opposite direction of most travelers. At midday they reached St. Mary's Station where a meal of bacon, fried bread, beans and coffee waited them while men unhooked the teams and hitched fresh horses and mules in their place. These animals would make the trip back to South Pass City the following morning.

St. Mary's Station was like most stage stops. A long, low, dirt-floored log building housed the station keeper and his help with rooms for the stage passengers to spend the night. Boards had been freighted up the trail from End of Track to be used in the construction of tables, chairs and beds. Behind the main building stood three outbuildings with a fence of upright logs to protect the stock. At each station there always seemed to be one or more emigrant trains arriving or leaving, and this proved to be true when Amy arrived. A caravan of twenty wagons, all ox-drawn, was just arriving.

Five miles on down the river the wagons turned right around a low ridge, and they could see Sweetwater Station in the distance.

Several tents, erected north of the corrals, garrisoned a small cavalry detachment and an infantry unit.

It was late afternoon when the wagons left Sweetwater Station, but now four infantry guards rode escort on uncomfortable perches atop the freight wagon.

Harry sensed Amy's concern and explained, "We're getting closer to the Platte. It's Sioux Country north of here. We'll have the army boys with us the rest of the way."

"The mountain range south of here seems to be getting taller," said Amy.

"That's Crook's Gap on the east end of Green Mountain. We could go through there, but there's no water the rest of the way, so we'll go on east and turn south through Whiskey Gap after we change horses on this side."

"Do we have to go through there in the dark?"

"I'm afraid so," he said, grimly.

"What time will we reach the railhead?"

"If all goes well, we should be there tomorrow afternoon."

She could tell they were climbing and could see the faint outline of a tall mountain range out the left window. She dropped off to sleep for short periods of time but awoke frequently with the lurching of the coach as its wheels struggled over the rocky bed. "No place to break an axle," she thought.

She slept until morning and awakened with a start, her head resting against Harry's shoulder. The stage had passed through Whiskey Gap and was well out on the flat plains country and making good time.

"We're not likely to see Indians now, are we, Harry?" she asked.

"No. Not likely. We would have seen them at dawn in the Gap."

"Will they send an escort out to meet us?"

"I doubt it," he said. "It should be clear sailing from here to End of Track.

CHAPTER NINETEEN

BENNIE'S BUNCH

Bennie was a middle-aged, fat man wearing a tan, felt, narrow brimmed hat with a sloppy, rounded crown. His dirty canvas pants, held up with suspenders, hadn't been washed since he bought them. His long, matted gray hair was getting in the way of his drink. His equally blowzy sidekick was sitting at the same table. Bennie wiped the back of his shirtsleeve across his mouth and peeked at his hole card, "And a hundred," he giggled. Squirming in his chair with obvious satisfaction with his stud poker hand, he fumbled through his stack of gold coins and pushed his bet to the center of the table with short stubby fingers. He looked at his partner, Henry Lee and winked.

"Why, you fat swindler, you switched that card!" said a thin-faced grader with hairy hands.

Round-faced and red-nosed, Bennie, flushed from too much rotgut whiskey and lack of sleep, peered through puffy lids and bloodshot eyes as anger raised the hairs on the back of his neck, and he said through clinched teeth, "You son-of-a-bitch!" His hand darted for his pistol.

A loud, roaring explosion beat Bennie to the draw. Henry Lee, tall, thin, darting-eyed-sidekick of Bennie, shot the grader through the table, blowing gold coins around the wooden deck.

The music and gaiety slowed for a few minutes as the body was dragged outside and dumped. "Let's go find a woman," said the killer. Dressed in a gray wool shirt, black pants held up with a belt six inches too long, its end dangled loosely through a crudely fashioned brass buckle, Henry Lee strode past the banjo player on his way out the door.

They stalked out of the big tent and into the ankle-deep dust where twenty-five tents stood.

"That'll teach the creep to call me a cheat!" puffed Bennie.

"You showed him, boss," said Henry Lee as they walked to one of the women's tents identified by a garter over the ridge pole.

Bennie gave the garter a twirl, opened the flap, "Damn! Nobody home!"

"I need a drink," said Henry Lee.

"Yea, not enough women in this camp," complained Bennie.

"Alfredo's down at Brent's saloon. He'll know where the women are," said Henry Lee. "Come on, boss."

Forty yards down the street, Brent's saloon and gambling hall glowed in the afternoon sun. A medley of discordant noises tumbled through the door while Bennie and Henry Lee shouldered their way into the crowd.

"Wouldn't you know it. Playin' faro with the best lookin' woman in the house. That's Alfredo!" whooped Henry Lee. "Remember all them women in El Paso? Alfredo sure can pick 'em."

Bennie, Henry Lee and Alfredo had drifted north with the cattle drives after the Civil War. But they hadn't worked too hard at it: Bennie hated dust, Henry hated work and

Alfredo liked women. They had hustled a living somehow.
All three had agreed that the best opportunity to present
itself in their lifetimes was these tent towns that followed
the railroad construction gangs. Liquor flowed freely while
gambling never stopped.

Now Henry Lee addressed Alfredo, "Hey, amigo! Ain't
you goin' to introduce us to the pretty lady?"

Alfredo looked up with a wide smile, "Sure, Henry Lee.
She is to be my wife. We will be married tonight."

"Ha! Where you goin' to find a parson in this pig-sty?"

"Plenty of preachers here. I hear folks praying all the
time," laughed Alfredo. "Pull up a chair and give the little
lady your money."

Alfredo was a handsome man, polite, well-mannered; he
just didn't like to work. Money had come easy to him,
sometime by the knife, sometime by the gun. But on every
occasion in a fair fight. He gazed intently at Bennie, "Some
good lookin' women down the street, Bennie, about a
hundred yards on the left."

Bennie, without answering Alfredo, motioned for Henry
Lee to follow, and together the two men walked back
through the crowd to the door.

"Didn't I tell you? Didn't I tell you Alfredo would know
where all the women were?" marveled Henry Lee with
deep admiration.

"That's about all he's good for," said Bennie.

"Ah, you're just jealous," sang Henry Lee as they entered
a tent with a stack of whiskey barrels at the entrance. A sign
painted on a barrel simply read, "Saloon".

"Faro, boys?" said the tough-looking woman.

"What else you deal?" asked Henry Lee.

"They are more expensive," she said.

"That's what we've come for," said Bennie; "we've got
the money."

A lieutenant at the poker table looked straight at Bennie

without smiling and said, "When your friend returns, meet me in my tent across the street."

"And?" asked Bennie.

"Business," said the lieutenant.

Thirty minutes later, across the street, Sampson, hearing a shuffling noise outside his tent called, "Come on in, boys. Have a seat," he said, holding open the flap of the tent.

Bennie had trouble squeezing into the narrow folding chair, but after settling himself as best he could said agitatedly, "What kind of job is it, lieutenant?"

Sampson poured three glasses full of dark whiskey, handed Bennie and Henry Lee each a drink, and then he proposed a toast, "Holdup."

"Ha! You soldier boys are supposed to protect people, not hold 'em up," said Henry Lee.

"Shut up," said Bennie, scoldingly, with a nasty look at Henry Lee. "Tell us more."

"You get ten men. I'll split fifty-fifty with you. Divide your share any way you want."

"How much do you expect?"

"A lot of money."

"Now I don't deal in generalities, lieutenant," said Bennie. "How much is a lot?"

"I told you I'd split half with you."

"Divided among ten men! It'll have to be a pile of money," smirked Bennie.

"Two hundred thousand." He paused, "In gold."

"Hot damn!" clapped Henry Lee.

"Ten men be enough?"

"Sure will; I've got a surprise for them."

"Anyone else with you?" wondered Bennie.

"Just a corporal. I need him for the gun."

"You pay him out of your cut!" Bennie glared. The

lieutenant nodded acceptance. "When do we split the gold?" Bennie asked.

"When I say so!"

"What's your plan?"

"I'll tell you tomorrow afternoon. I've got a packstring of mules with supplies. Come riding a good horse. I don't want to see a nag in the bunch," said Sampson. "And," he added, "bring a big canteen. No whiskey! And I mean, not a drop." He lowered his voice to accent his military mien. "Do I make myself clear?"

Bennie shifted his ponderous frame in the flimsy chair threatening its collapse and in an utterance a little too strained from the anticipation of all that gold, said, "I admire a man who likes to give orders and I can see you're such a man. I'll have ten of the toughest men who ever rode a trail. Six of 'em are in my bunch right now. Four more won't be hard to round up in this camp." Bennie's voice, steadied with use, grew more confident while he measured the lieutenant through narrow slits in his swollen face. "My men will 'Sir' you to hell-and-back, follow any rule you set, ride from here to California, and do your dirty work, but, Sir," his voice lowered in the manner of the lieutenant, "there had better be gold at the end of the day. Do I make myself clear?"

The lieutenant changed his demeanor, rose quickly to his feet and in a jovial mood poured another round of whiskey and said, "Now that we understand each other," he lifted his glass, "to our success, gentlemen!"

Bennie relaxed, his flushed face contented, said, "Until tomorrow, then, lieutenant." He rose laboriously, with a wheeze and said to Henry Lee, "Come on, we have work to do."

By morning, Bennie had gathered the meanest bunch of cutthroats imaginable. They were drifters, who follow the gaming tables and loose women; they just stayed ahead of the law and killed for a living. They were a slovenly group with battered hats and unwashed clothes that looked like they had slept in them for weeks and probably had. A goateed man with a receding hairline, thin eyebrows, narrow hooked nose, had worn a long duster in spite of the heat; a thick chested, muscular man, thirty years old, had ridden a big buckskin all the way from Alabama to escape the ravages of the Civil War; two graders, dissatisfied with the back breaking work had looked forward to easier labor, and jumped at Bennie's offer of $1,000 in gold for two days' work. The lieutenant would know Bennie could really pick 'em.

The lieutenant wore his cavalry trousers with the stripe down the side. He had brushed and polished his boots shiny bright that morning, but now they were covered with thick alkali dust. He had discarded his tunic to replace it with a fringed buckskin jacket. A wide belt held his 1860 Army Colt .44. He wore his tan cavalry hat with its brim turned up in front, which exposed his dark sun-browned face, accentuating his black hair, moustache and long sideburns. He had spent a sleepless night, his mind going over and over the planned ambush. Now, Sampson looked around his tent for any last minute item and picked up his field glasses off the cot. Throwing back the tent flap, he walked to his dark bay horse and mounted. At a slow walk, he traveled to the end of the street, joined Bennie and his bunch and led them north down the river one mile where they swam their horses to the west bank.

While they were scurrying up the bank, five miles on down the river from Brownsville, the corporal had assembled the Mountain Gatling Gun. It commanded the trail as it approached a narrow declivity bordering the river. A year before, in Kansas, the corporal was a member of one of the lucky gun-crews that actually got to fire a Gatling Gun, but only one magazine full of ammunition could be spared. The gun had jammed three times. "I hope this thing works," he thought, testing the crank on the ten barreled contrivance. He pried the lid off a wooden box which contained rimfire .58 caliber cartridges, loaded them one at a time into the gun's magazine and fitted the magazine upright into the receiver. He looked up the river, across the scorched sagebrush and saw the dust column of Lieutenant Sampson and his band as they drew nearer. The corporal waited, nervously toying with the wooden handle on the crank of the gun.

In a few minutes, Lieutenant Sampson, at the head of the column of men stopped his horse near the corporal and his gun emplacement.

"Everything ready, corporal?"

"Yes, sir!"

"Any sign of the wagons?"

"Yes, sir. About three miles away. You can see their dust through the glasses." He turned toward the northwest and pointed.

"Now remember, reminded the leader, gazing directly at Bennie, "leave the stagecoach alone. It will be in the lead. Three passengers on the stage are with us. They'll take care of the driver and the guard. Understand?" he asked, crisply.

"It's your command, lieutenant," agreed Bennie sardonically.

"Hide the horses in that grove of cottonwood up the river. One man stay with them. And keep them out of sight! No shooting until after the Gatling Gun opens up. Now spread out and keep down."

At the same time, a mile and a half across the sagebrush flats the wheels of the freight wagon clattered over the rocks as it lurched and protested behind the stagecoach. The stage closed fast with the wagon following thirty yards behind. The four soldiers jostled atop the loaded freighter.

A soldier screamed a warning, "Ambushers!" The rest had no time to react.

In the stagecoach Harry threw himself across Amy's lap, pulled his holstered pistol and fired it up through the forward panel where the driver rode.

A staccato of gunfire reverberated against the cedar ridge across the river; wounded mules screamed; then all was quiet.

"You son-of-a-bitch. You weren't supposed to shoot up the stage!" Harry Montagu screeched from inside the coach. The stage door opened, and a body fell out.

Amy Stafford's face, drained of color and pinched with fright, quivered as she said in a trembling voice, "Harry, are you all right?"

"Not a scratch, but these two are done," he said, pushing the other dead man out the door.

Back in the rocks the lieutenant ordered Bennie, "Send someone to bring up the horses."

Turning to Henry Lee, Bennie, sweating profusely snapped, "Get to it!"

Without a sound, Henry Lee jogged up the river to the grove of trees where the horses were tied and in a few minutes returned in a cloud of dust accompanied by the horse guard. The band of outlaws now rode to the stagecoach.

"Where's the gold?" demanded the lieutenant.

"In the flour barrels."

The outlaws swarmed over the wagon and kicked the barrels out of the end. They fell against the rocks and burst, spewing flour in all directions. Now with the sacks of gold, stacked and counted, the lieutenant faced Bennie.

"Twenty-four, lieutenant. Is that all of them?"

"That's correct," interjected Amy.

"Who's the dame?" glared Henry Lee.

"Bring up the mules," ordered Sampson, as he untied the tops of several sacks.

"Two sacks on each side," he continued, shaking out a handful of yellow gold dust.

"Beautiful!" grinned a bandit.

They packed six mules quickly. A pair of heavy canvas aparejos with leather reinforced corners slung across the sawbuck pack-saddle of each mule waited to be filled. The corporal uncoiled a rawhide lash rope and tossed one end on the ground to his right. He laid the rope between the crossbucks and threw the opposite end with the lash cinch to his helper on the off side who handed it back to him under the belly of the mule where he hooked it and pulled it up tight. Two twists taken on top of the load with the rope pulled up through formed the diamond. He handed the fixed rope to his helper who caught the corner of the right rear pack and continued under the load to the front, and then to the left side of the mule, pulling hard as they went. A final jerk of the rope and the load was tied securely.

"Fine mules, Cap'n. I hope you've got water for them," mused Bennie.

"You want to take the gun?" called the corporal.

"No! Throw it in the river. It will slow us down," replied the lieutenant.

"Any of your men hurt, Bennie?"

"One man killed. No one else touched."

They rolled the Gatling Gun to the edge of the Platte and pushed it down the hill where it gathered speed and was airborne for thirty feet before striking the water.

"Let's get moving! I'm sure they heard the shooting up the river," said the lieutenant. He turned his horse north along the stream.

The twelve men and one woman stopped to water the animals two miles on downstream. The river turned sharply to the east around the northern edge of Cedar Ridge. At this point they abandoned the river, rode into the Haystack Mountains where the rocky slopes made it more difficult for tracking. The lieutenant knew that the wind and darkness were his allies. "An Eastern dude fresh off the train could follow this herd," he thought.

"Be dark in another two hours," stated Harry. "Are we going to hole up in those mountains?"

"We're going to make them think so," said Lieutenant Sampson.

They continued on a northerly course for fifteen miles around the upper end of the Sand Dunes. The wind blew ferociously, driving sand and dirt into their faces and making visibility impossible. Darkness consumed them. "Table Mountain must be in front of us," thought Sampson. They paused to water the string and stretch their legs.

"I'm ready to call it a day," complained one of Bennie's bunch.

"It's nine o'clock. The moon will be up in a couple of hours. It's a long way to water, so fill your canteens," ordered Sampson.

"What the hell! We going to ride all night?" moaned Bennie.

They headed down Stone Creek in a southwesterly direction around the northern edge of the Sand Dunes. After continuing on this course for about five miles, Henry Lee kicked his horse alongside Clark's, "Hell, Cap'n, this will take us into the desert."

"That's the plan."

"But, there's no water!"

"You ever been out there?"

"No."

"Then come along. That's where the gold's going."

CHAPTER TWENTY

ACROSS SEPARATION CREEK

"Cold this morning, boys," shivered Jedediah. He dropped the flap of the tent. "Stars are out. Going to be a hot one by noon.

"How's the stock doing?" inquired Howie, as he poured Jed a cup of coffee.

"What say we get to packin'?"

The mules, brushed down and grained, were ready for saddling. Jed and Howie tightened the cinches and commenced loading each animal. Two men to the pack made quick work for these frontiersmen. Jedediah packed the grain mules by first fashioning a barrel sling on the sawbuck packsaddle. He found the middle of the sling rope, threw a half hitch over the front sawbuck with half the rope on each side of the mule, and next formed a loop in the front by passing the end down the center of the crossbuck and through the rear crossbuck where he formed a second loop and continued the rope back through the rear buck and out at the center of the packsaddle. Jimmy lifted up a large sack of grain and he pulled both the forward and rear loops tight around the load with the center rope pulled up under and then passed over to the off side. Howie formed the sling on his side and balanced the second sack of grain in a like manner. Jimmy threw a diamond hitch over the load. Each mule carried a light load except the grain mules, which carried three-hundred pounds apiece. Two mules each carried two empty twenty-five gallon barrels.

In the dark early morning the river camp remained quiet while the four figures quickly went about their work. Brownsville slumbered at this early hour, but here and there a light glowed and a tinkle of sound faintly bounced along the river. The army slept as the column swam the Platte. The pack mules, led across one at a time and held in a group until all the animals were on the west bank, were tied tail to halter rope in groups of threes with each man leading three mules. What had begun as spirited jockeying for position by the mules soon settled into a methodical ground eating pace toward the west and their watering hole at the springs.

They reached Rawlins Springs by sunup. It was already getting warm as they watered the stock and filled the barrels. Numerous antelope grazed near the springs and buffalo tracks covered the marshy banks. Four mule deer, one young buck and three does watched as the column moved away from the water hole.

Two hours later, twelve miles west of the springs they crossed the divide and picked up Separation Creek. It was almost dry at this time of the year, but there was enough water for the stock and for their canteens.

"Pretty dry from here on," said Jimmy, unbuttoning his gray flannel shirt.

The mules, tailed with a break string in case they got in trouble, trotted briskly behind Howie. Jimmy rode ahead about a mile. The other two men were on each flank.

"Not much chance of being surprised in this wide open

country," thought Howie. Still, they had taken turns stopping to glass the country side. The Sioux had often crossed from the Sweetwater to the Overland Trail right through here. "This must have been about where Brown and his cavalry escort had run into the Sioux raiding party which led to Brown's death."

Their dust trail, visible for five miles during the morning hours now was dispersed by the gusting wind. As the afternoon wore on, the winds picked up to gusts of forty to fifty miles an hour, blowing out of the west, straight into their faces. They rode forty-five miles, turned north into the desert, and looked for a place to camp.

As darkness drew nearer, the sunset changed; the winds calmed, and the four men sought shelter for the night in a sagebrush-covered draw. They unpacked their mules and unsaddled their horses. One man slipped a full nosebag of grain over the ears of each animal. Later, after they finished the grain, Jimmy watered the stock using a canvas bucket. He hobbled them and turned them loose to graze. Not much feed, but as tired as they were, they wouldn't stray far. Over in the draw, Charles built a small fire in the bottom of a dry stream bed and prepared their supper of fried bread, bacon, stew from dried buffalo meat, dried apples and coffee.

"What do you expect they are doing for water?" asked Howie.

"Same as us," answered Jed.

"Yeah, they probably packed it with them," agreed Charles.

"Hell, they're most likely having a beer up in South Pass right now," laughed Jimmy.

"And counting their gold!" added Charles.

"How much you say they got, Howie?" inquired Jed.

"Twenty-four sacks of the stuff. Each sack about forty pounds. That's almost a thousand pounds. It assayed twelve dollars an ounce. That's about two hundred thousand."

"What would you do with that much gold, Jed?" queried Charles.

"I'd take me a trip down to New Orleans, like Howie did, and get all mushy over a dark-eyed woman," he chuckled.

"You'd get more trouble than you bargained for, I promise you!" suggested Howard.

Each man laid out his bedroll around the campfire and prepared for sleep on the high desert plain.

Howard drew his rifle from its leather scabbard and announced, "I'll take the first watch. We'll change every two hours. I'll be on the ridge about fifty yards down the draw."

CHAPTER TWENTY-ONE

WAR PARTY

"When do we divvy up the gold?" demanded Bennie, angrily flinging the rest of his coffee into the fire.

"I told you. When I say so, not before."

"Come on, man," whined Henry Lee. "You didn't say nothin' about chasing around this damn desert!"

"Fifty-fifty, remember?" reminded Bennie. "We've got the gold; I'm ready for my cut."

The lieutenant was losing control, and drawn faces around the campfire watched the showdown with an expectation of violence.

"Dry camp. Those mules haven't had water in over eight hours. I'm getting out of here, and I'm taking my gold with me," growled Bennie. He picked up one pannier with eighty pounds of the dust.

"Drop it!" intoned Sampson in the laconic voice of a man used to giving orders and expecting them obeyed.

"Well, soldier boy, I've taken all the crap I'm gonna take from you!" Bennie said, as his hand darted for his gun.

His head dropped, as if to look at the hole above his belt buckle. He never cleared leather.

"Henry Lee?" offered the lieutenant from a crouched position with the still smoking .44 pointed at the tall thin man's chest.

"Not me, boss! Whatever you say," as he showed his empty hands.

"Now, believe this. All of you. The army is patrolling all along the Sweetwater. To the east is Fort Laramie. And you can bet your share of the gold that Howard Prescott is organizing the toughest band of men that money can buy."

"Who the hell's Howard Prescott?" inquired a Mexican vaquero, as he spat a wad of chewing tobacco into the fire.

"He's the owner of that freight line you just shot up," volunteered Amy.

"Well, little lady, word around Brownsville is that you were on your way to marry him," said a mean-looking gambler with a goatee.

"Seems like you're running with about everybody," chimed a third.

Amy flashed a look at the lieutenant as Harry's face covered with resentment.

"Why don't we split up? They can't follow us all," interrupted the man with the goatee.

"That's just what we'll do, but we'll hole up for two days here in the desert," said Clark Sampson.

"You're mad! These mules won't live that long. We might not either," he added.

"Harry, fill them in," said the lieutenant.

"Thirty miles west of here we have a wagon with five fifty-gallon barrels of water and two hundred pounds of grain. There's even a jug or two of whiskey," said Harry.

"Yahoo!" shouted Henry Lee, "Now that's more like it."

"There's food and a sack of cooking utensils on that wagon. We'll be safe and undetected. We rest up for a

couple of days, and then ride out in different directions,"
said the lieutenant.

The men hadn't paid much attention to Amy because
they were preoccupied with the long night's ride and the
lack of water. Her braided hair, in a tight pigtail down the
middle of her back, reached the bottom of her fawn colored
deerskin jacket. Her black broadcloth riding skirt, smudged
with dust, needed laundering. Beads of perspiration trickled
rivulets of dirty streaks down her face and neck. She yearned
for a bath and the opportunity to wash her hair.

"Dirty work for such a handsome woman," said the vaquero.

"Alfredo! You take the first watch," ordered the lieutenant,
"We won't be here more than two, three hours. Sunup soon.
We'll be out of here before it gets hot."

Later, the wind blew a flicker of flame to the dying fire.
Dark figures, covered with blankets, turned restlessly,
seeking comfort.

"All quiet, corporal?" whispered the lieutenant.

"Coyotes getting closer, sir."

At that moment a four note yelp echoed softly down
the draw. "Better wake the men."

The corporal scurried among sleeping figures whispering,
"Indians!"

First light hinted up the draw, but to the west, darkness
prevailed. A faint bark drifted out of the east. All in camp
were now wide awake.

Erosion had worn deep gashes in the edges of the arroyo
which afforded cover for the defenders. The lieutenant
saw Amy huddled in one of them, Harry at her side. Wide
awake, she held her Deringer at the ready.

Minutes passed while all members of the lieutenant's
party, fully alert, strained to hear a scraping noise, a horse's
hoof, a coyote's yip. Clark Sampson used his glasses, searched
the horizon, the draws, the escarpment to the south and
watched streaks of light increase in the east. "Just a few

more minutes," he thought. "Corporal," he said softly,
"take two men and gather the stock. Be quick!"

Harry, down the draw, sighted down his rifle barrel.
He still could not see his sights. As the men returned with
the horses, the horses bolted at the startling boom of musket
fire from a large war party that appeared from a gulley to
the east. A shower of arrows came from the shadows of the
west. A wounded man screamed loudly, tore frantically at
an arrow embedded deeply into his hip.

Amid the confusion of milling horses and clouds of dust,
the lieutenant tried vainly to direct fire. The Indians
retreated to a low ridge of sand dunes, out of rifle range,
to demonstrate their superiority.

Two men were dead. A third would not see the sunrise.
Henry Lee squinted into the darkness and said, "Now
what, Cap'n?

"It's their deck." said the lieutenant. He focused his field
glasses on the enemy gathered along the escarpment bordering
the sand dunes. He could see the war party, armed with
single shot muzzle loaders on their war ponies reloading
their rifles. Each brave had his bow and a quiver full of
arrows. These were short, powerful bows made of mountain
ash with strings of buffalo sinew. They would abandon their
musket and favor the bow and the lance with the next rush.
The chief raised his feathered battle standard to signal the
attack. The warriors bent low over the outstretched necks
of the horses and flew over the ground with great skill.
The gunfire from the Spencers and Henrys was too much
for them, however, as their horses fell under them. They
turned to regroup.

"They're gonna' starve us out!" blurted the gambler.

"We've got food. We haven't got water."

"Give them the woman!" screamed the goateed ambusher.

"I'll break your damn neck," slurred Harry, as he dove
for the man.

The lieutenant stepped between them, "Knock it off. We need every gun."

"They're killing our mules, sir. Two down now," reported the corporal.

"How many head of stock left?"

"Twenty four. Four with arrows in 'em. Twenty sound."

"Cut loose all but ten head."

"Sir?"

"Cut them loose!" demanded the lieutenant. "Keep six mules. They'll take the horses and they may just leave us alone."

From the ridge, the Chief watched the fleeing horses. With a wave of his hand, a small party rode to retrieve them. The raiding party slowly disappeared over the crest.

"They've gone, Cap'n?" hoped Henry Lee.

"I wouldn't bet on it," droned Sampson, peering intently through his field glasses.

And now it was late afternoon; the blistering heat of the sun faded to the west. The choking dust and drying wind had begun to crack their lips, tempers flared, nerves frayed and fatigue had begun to take its toll on their nerves.

"Saddle the stock," ordered Sampson.

With a flurry of activity, saddles cinched and panniers secured, someone yelled, "Take cover!"

On the ridge, a long line of braves sat watching the activity. The Chief stared impassively for several minutes, then turned, and led his band toward the Sweetwater.

"Four walk, four ride; we'll take turns every half mile," stated Clark.

There were eight left in their party. They scraped shallow graves for the dead and formed a crude cover by piling what few rocks they could find over the top. The coyotes would dig them up by midnight.

By sunset the straggling column paused, in the afterglow, exhausted, on a low mound of sand and sagebrush.

The lieutenant looked to the west with his field glasses. "Do you see it, Harry?"

"No, Clark, but I see the ravine it's in," responded Harry. He scanned the dimness with his glasses. "There," he pointed. "Three or four more miles."

"I can't go no further," gasped goatee as he fell face first in the sand.

"Okay, we'll double up the mules. Everybody rides," said Clark.

They repacked the gold, eight sacks to the mule. The four horses weren't doing well.

"Pull the saddles off the horses. We'll come back after them tomorrow."

It had grown dark, but they could still see in the twilight.

"It has to be here somewhere," complained Harry.

"There it is!" pointed Alfredo.

They kicked their exhausted mounts down the draw. The wagon and its load was intact. One man threw the canvas tarp back and opened the water barrels. Water brought quick new life to the haggard group. A barrel of grain replenished the stock.

Amy splashed water on her face and rolled out her blankets, totally exhausted. She had slept for two hours, and then awakened when the lieutenant offered her a bowl of thick soup. "This will perk you up a little," he stated. "I'm sorry about all this, Amy. I truly didn't know you were on that stage."

"Harry didn't tell you?"

"No."

"I'll try to get you out of this," he promised.

After a period of thirty minutes the camp was sound asleep except for one guard who nodded his head and tried, unsuccessfully, to stay awake.

Awakened by the wind, Harry stirred the fire, put on a pot of coffee, watched the others sleep, and smoked a cigarette while the coffee boiled. He poured himself a cup, drank it with his second cigarette, poured more coffee into a second cup, walked to Amy's bed and gently nudged her shoulder with his boot. "You going to sleep all day?"

"Thanks, Harry." New life, restored after a long night's sleep was evident about the midmorning campfire. The stock had found a few pickens on down the arroyo and grazed, contented, along its low hillside.

Amy's strength had returned. She took a canvas bucket of water over into the next draw. She removed her blouse and laid it over some greasewood, placed her double-barreled Deringer on her hat and looked at her breasts, which had become caked with sand and grit. She splashed water on her hair and lathered it with a bar of soap, rinsing it as best she could. She then washed her face and let the water run down her breasts. She soaped her hands, rubbed the foam over her breasts, and leaned over the bucket to flick water over her chest. She dried her breasts and noted the nipples were erect from the stimulation. She looked up and saw the goateed man, leering at her in anticipation.

"I'll dry them for you," he offered, huskily.

She reached for her Deringer, but he knocked it to the sand, and stepped on it with his boot.

"No need for that," he panted. He grabbed her wrist and started to pull her toward him.

She drew back, thrusting her breasts ever so slightly, "Maybe you'll want to help me finish my bath?" she said, slowly unbuttoning her skirt. With a twist of her hips the skirt slipped over her mound of dark hair. She pulled the Remington Vest Pocket .22 rimfire from her garter holster and shot him between the eyes. The entire camp came running and arrived as she finished buttoning a clean blouse.

"He got more than he wanted."

CHAPTER TWENTY-TWO

PURSUIT

"I'll go north and check out Crook's Gap," stated Jimmy, finishing his coffee.

Not liking the way one of the mule's load was balanced, Howard quickly untied the diamond and repacked the panniers. He turned to the group and said, "Camp will be moved ten miles straight west. Charles, you probe southwest. Jedediah, northeast. Don't take any chances. You find them, you return to camp. Watch your hair!"

They gave each horse and mule five gallons of water that morning and turned one pack mule loose. It followed them for awhile and finally drifted east.

This would be another day of smothering dust. The mirage from both wind and heat was extreme. A man's eyes played tricks on him. This high mountain desert had meager vegetation, its barren landscape parched. In winter, 50 below temperatures were not uncommon, and men sought shelter to avoid it. Even in July cold nights occurred,

while by day, temperatures reached nearly one hundred
degrees. Prickly pear cactus grew as did scanty sagebrush.
In the gullies, where drifting snow was trapped in winter,
the sagebrush had grown taller. There were no trees, only
low growing brush in the deeper draws such as cottonthorn
horsebrush, scrub cedar, sagebrush, greasewood and other
species such as saltbush, winterfat, sagewort, rabbitbrush,
spiny hopsage, bitterbrush and mountain mahogany. The
coyote and the wolf fed on rabbits and mice. Antelope were
rather plentiful, and buffalo had crossed those plains to
better grazing. There are grasses on that desert, many of them
in fact, such as Indian ricegrass, bottlebrush squirreltail,
western wheatgrass, basin wildrye, sandberg bluegrass, inland
saltgrass and foxtail, but for large herds of buffalo the
pickens were scanty, so they drifted on east of Elk Mountain
to graze the rich Laramie Plains where the grass was deep
and the succulent grama grass grew.

Jedediah chewed on a piece of jerky, twirled a stem of
wildrye and glassed the gentle slopes in front of him. He
saw tracks traversing the hill. Putting the glasses in his saddle
bag, he urged his horse along at a walk. There were at least
thirty sets of tracks made by unshod horses, all heading
easterly. He had followed them for five miles, and then he
saw them turn south toward Bridger's Pass. "Definitely
Indians," he realized. "That lieutenant would be riding a
horse with shoes." He turned back the way he had come,
stopping in a draw to rest his horse and smoke a pipe. He
watched a herd of buffalo being stalked by a small pack of
wolves. "They must have seen that calf limping," he thought.
Focusing his glasses on the herd, which was nervously milling
about and testing the wind for sign, he picked out a one
year old buffalo bull-calf dragging its right hind leg.
Jedediah's first experience watching a wolf-pack hunt was
along the Missouri River at the age of twelve. A small herd
of whitetail deer, driven onto the ice, was quickly dispatched

by the powerful wolves. He suddenly realized that he hadn't been home in over ten years. He had been south as far as Santa Fe and had wintered in Taos, but he had not been back to St. Louis where he was born. He had grown up watching hunting parties form for trips to the Rockies, where there were beaver to trap and buffalo to kill. And he had seen the Indian maidens so pretty that they would make most men want to stay forever. When he was a youngster, the covered wagons lined up for a mile in the streets near his house. As they pulled out for the west, he had cried to go with them.

In 1853, at the age of twenty, he had wintered with the Indians along the Seeds-kee-dee and trapped beaver to trade for tobacco and guns. He admired the Indian and accepted his ways. He was saddened to see the Indian lands being encroached by the white man even though he was one. The buffalo were fewer, and the white men more numerous. After the Mormons began their trek to Utah in 1846, gold was discovered in California at Sutter's Mill in 1848, and the migration of the white man began in earnest. Tens of thousands of people swarmed up the Platte to the consternation of the Indians. By the time Jedediah ascended the Platte in 1853, deep mutilating scars laced the landscape along the trail to the west. Iron wagonwheels dug deep wounds into the ground while wind and rain completed the erosion of the fragile soil whose roots had successfully withstood thousands of years of nature's incessant battering. But now the Indian was being brutal, mutilating their victims. And how could you blame them after events like Sand Creek? Those folks south of here had been inflamed by Indian raids into offering twenty-five dollars' bounty for each Indian scalp brought in. Still, he loved this desolation and its simple ethic. He had learned in his lifetime, that nature, while bountiful, was unforgiving to the careless; unintelligible to the ill-prepared, and relentless to the weak.

The challenges nature offered and the adventures gained were reward enough for Jedediah.

He was dozing in the afternoon sun when he realized he must get moving. He emptied one of his canteens into a canvas bucket and watered his horse. He would follow the Indian tracks back into the west.

Meanwhile, to the south, Charles had traveled to within sight of the rail bed. He saw dugouts built along the grading where work gangs found shelter. The crews had moved on west. Empty kegs that were once full of spikes lay half buried in the sand. Supplies to this point had been brought up by wagon and team. He continued along the road for fifteen miles and finally turned north across flat desert land to return to camp.

At Crook's Gap Jimmy had detected no sign of travelers. He had gone west along the Mormon Trail for six miles, and then south eighteen miles to Bastard Butte. The Mormons had stuck to the north side of the Platte River thus hoping to avoid contact with other travelers, but the trails were reversed over this stretch of the Sweetwater with the Mormon Trail south of the river and the Oregon Trail north of the river. Three miles to the east he crossed their tracks. They were headed west.

There was plenty of water up in Crook's Gap, but most of it was from sulpher springs and alkali streams. He had found fresh water for his canteens and horse, however, at a series of small lakes one mile north of the Continental Divide and eight miles north of Bastard Butte. As he continued to ride west, he knew they were out there somewhere, and he knew who would find them, but this band sure slipped the cavalry. Watching a lone horseman come out of the south, he pulled his field glasses out of his saddle bags for a closer look but the distance was too great, and he couldn't make him out. He swung to the ground and laid prone for a steadier look. The mirage was impossible.

Distorted waves crossed his field of vision at almost a right angle. He laid his horse on the ground and waited as the rider worked his way up the gentle slope.

"Jedediah. How goes it?"

"Fine, Jimmy. I saw you through my glasses about thirty minutes ago. Couldn't make you out, but I was sure it was you." He pointed toward the ground, "These tracks, about twenty-five head, I make it."

Jimmy nodded agreement. They gazed west toward the sunset. "Be dark in an hour," said Jedediah.

"Yup. Your horse had water?"

"Not much, Jim."

"I've got two full canteens. I watered my horse a few hours ago."

"My one canteen is still full," said Jedediah.

"We'll give two canteens of water to your horse and save the other for some night coffee."

"Hell of a band of Indians I've been backtrackin'," said Jedediah.

"Don't look good for that bunch," frowned Jim.

They tracked west for as long as there was light to see and then camped for the night. They had enough grain for this evening and tomorrow morning.

Coffee, jerky and dried apples tasted pretty good as the desert cold surrounded the camp.

"What do you make of it, Jed?"

"Indians probably bushwhacked 'em."

"No, I mean about this whole affair. It don't stack up."

"How you figure?"

"Why would Howie allow all that gold on the same trip with his fiancée?"

"I don't know, Jim. Five dollar beaver is about all I need! I can trade a beaver plew for five pounds of powder."

"That's what I was thinkin'. Hell, I got more woman at Fort Laramie than Howie will ever see!" he laughed.

Jimmy and Jedediah had each spent a long day, but each had picked up the trail of the outlaws. They would be up before dawn following the band to the west.

There were a million stars in the July sky as the night noises punctuated their reminiscing. Jimmy produced a small flask of whiskey that they shared until gone. "I'll call you in two hours, Jed."

The following morning, after six hours' sleep, Jimmy stirred up the fire. "Enough water for one pot of coffee," he said, awakening Jedediah, while blowing life into the fire.

They could barely see the horses down the draw about fifty yards. "Be light soon," said Jedediah.

While the coffee finished boiling, Jimmy peered into the southwest. "Howie's camp can't be more'n fifteen, twenty miles," he said. He reached for his field glasses and looked for a full minute. "Ravens, straight west about five miles."

They washed the buffalo jerky down with hot coffee and mounted their ponies. Riding nearer, they could make out the rocks of several graves. Coyotes had tried to uncover them, but so far without luck. Jimmy circled the battle site. Then he saw the tracks.

"Indians left to the southeast. Four horses, and six mules headed west. Four men walking."

Jedediah looked toward the southeast. "Gave them over half their stock."

"Yeah and four people," said Jimmy. "I wonder if the woman's alive."

"She'd have to be a hell of a broad," marveled Jedediah.

Jimmy turned his horse toward the west. "Let's find Howard and Charles."

They continued for about eight miles. Jimmy looked at Jedediah. "Straight as a string. They're not trying to hide their trail."

The two men turned south knowing the trail would be easy to find again. From time to time they stopped to scan the horizon looking for Howard and Charles. Crossing several sets of horse and mule tracks, Jimmy pointed to the northwest and said, "These are the tracks of Howard and the packstring. He can't be far ahead."

Urging their horses at a faster pace, they found Howie in a pretty good camp, for the desert. "Hello, Howard. Charles. How you doing?" greeted Jedediah.

"Good to see you two," answered Howie.

About fifteen miles south of the battle site, he had found a small spring with enough water to conserve their two twenty-five gallon barrels. The two men watered their horses and gave them an extra ration of grain.

"Any luck?" asked Richfield.

"Found where they fought a battle with Indians. Four graves. Ten head trailed west. Four people walking," commented Jimmy.

"Probably seven or eight alive," continued Jed; "they either had half their stock stolen, or they gave them up."

"Any sign of Amy?" wondered Howard.

"No sign," said Jimmy.

"I covered south to the railbed. Nothing there," said Charles. He stirred a kettle of beans that had cooked most of the night and morning. He added chili powder, salt, dried onion and jerky to the pot and turned to the reflector oven full of biscuits. The oven was made out of thin sheet iron by a blacksmith at Brownsville. A smaller kettle of dried apples simmered over the fire. A large skillet, jammed full of sizzling bacon needed attention. He turned to the group, "Get your plates!"

When they had eaten all they could hold and drunk several cups of coffee, Charles and Howard saddled the stock.

"You boys relax; we'll take care of the chores."

Late in the afternoon they crossed the tracks. "One day ahead of us?" wondered Howard.

"Two at the most," said Jimmy.

"They're exhausted. They can't travel far," Jedediah said.

"They're all dead if they haven't found water," said Charles.

"There they are," pointed Jimmy.

"Have they seen us?" queried Howard.

"I don't think so."

"Getting too dark to do much now."

"Can you see the girl?" asked Howie.

All four men glassed the wagon and campsite.

"She's near the wagon. Looks like her bed is under it," stated Charles.

"They have a whole damn wagon full of water!" exclaimed Howie. "Where in hell did they get it?"

"It's only thirty miles to South Pass City," reminded Jimmy.

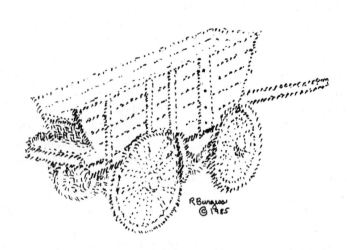

CHAPTER TWENTY-THREE

WHISKEY'S GONE

It's astonishing what water can do for a man who needs it. That wagon, with its precious cargo, had made them forget the gold. They had slept much of the second day from the effects of fatigue and whiskey. Their horses had grazed lazily, and no one strayed far from camp. They had formed a tarpaulin lean-to, erected against the wagon, and made a large fire pit, surrounded by rocks, and formed into a keyhole shape, and strap iron ripped from the wagon box laid over the back half formed for a cooking surface. An iron rod from the tail gate of the wagon had served as a spit across the front half of the fireplace for roasting freshly killed antelope haunches. A large pot of coffee had simmered day and night.

"That stale water tastes pretty damn good with a little corn mixed in it," grinned Henry Lee.

"Whiskey's 'bout gone, and I think we should be too," said a muscular, thick chested outlaw. He had a big Dragoon horse pistol in his hand and waved the group against the

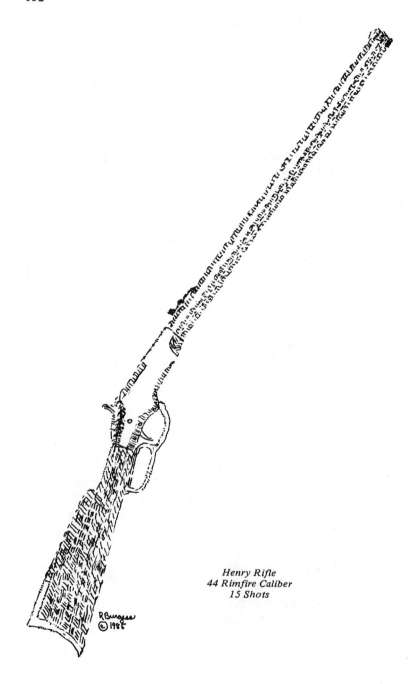

Henry Rifle
44 Rimfire Caliber
15 Shots

wagon. "I'm leaving. The girl goes with me. If I see so much as a dust trail, I'll kill her. You believe that don't you, lieutenant? Sir!" he screeched. He pushed the barrel of the heavy pistol under the lieutenant's chin.

"I believe you. Just don't hurt her," he said in a low voice.

"Now, little lady, throw your Deringer in the water barrel and fetch two horses and two mules," he said waving the girl toward the horses.

"Alfredo! You pack 'em. No tricks, comprendo?"

"What you waiting for? Get the other mule packed!" he shouted at Alfredo.

"You already got your share," complained Harry.

"I'm taking the woman's cut too. Lessen' you fellars think she ain't got one coming? Well? I didn't think you'd mind."

"Leave us some canteens," pleaded Henry Lee.

"You've got one apiece. Besides, you can hunker right here and drink them barrels dry!"

Mounting his horse, the outlaw turned to Harry. "If I see a speck of dust, she won't have no chest to button them purdy shirts on. Savvy?"

The lieutenant, Harry, Henry Lee, Alfredo and the others stood silently while the outlaw led the mules toward the Sweetwater with Amy riding at the rear. Sampson and the others watched them gradually pass out of sight behind a low ridge of sand dunes.

Lieutenant Sampson walked to his horse and began saddling it. He slammed his Spencer through the saddle horn boot and jerked the cinch latigo up tight. With a burlap sack he rubbed down the back of a mule and threw a heavy hair pad on its back and then the packsaddle. He buckled the chest strap and then the britchen strap.

"We gonna follow 'em, Cap'n?" asked Henry Lee.

"Hell no, we're not going to follow them!" he said angrily.

"Where we going?" asked Harry.

"I don't give a damn where you go. I suggest we split the gold right now."

"I think we better stick together," said the corporal. "That pair won't make it to the river. Some brave will have that pretty woman staked to his robe come nightfall."

The lieutenant led up another mule and tied it to the wheel of the wagon as he began packing it.

"Hombre! There ain't enough horses for all five of us!" complained Alfredo.

"That's right, pard. You want to make it four?"

The vaquero tipped his sombrero for a pregnant pause, then thought the better of it.

"Ride them out or leave the gold. Your choice. This cut leaves you two sacks apiece. That's eighty pounds."

"You're keeping eight sacks for yourself?" whined Henry Lee.

"That's right," said the lieutenant. He mounted his horse and led the two mules toward the Green.

As the events began to dawn on the remaining men, they hastily set to sorting and packing their panniers.

"We'll take turns riding," said Harry. He stepped in the saddle. "Tie the canteens on the mules. Get your rifles, and let's go!"

Alfredo, Henry Lee, and the corporal scurried around the wagon gathering up their gear and at a jog fell in behind Harry.

CHAPTER TWENTY-FOUR

CLOSING

"Well, I'll be damned! There's a barrel of water left," Charles announced as they rode up to the abandoned wagon at the deserted outlaw camp.

"They were in such a hell of a hurry it's a wonder they took the rest of the gold," remarked Jimmy drily.

Ashes from the outlaws' campfire blew, blue and gray, across the reddish sand. Howard bent over the fire and tested the ashes for heat. "Jedediah, you know every gully along the Sweetwater," he implored, first with a look north along the trail taken by Amy and the outlaw, and with a look at his friend.

"I'll take four canteens and no pack animal," he responded. He dumped some grain on the lowered tailgate of the wagon for his horse to eat. "That pilgrim won't make good time with those pack mules and that girl. He'll be looking at his backtrail and counting his gold. I should catch them by dark." He unbridled his horse, unsaddled him, rubbed down his back with a sack and left him with the grain.

"Coffee pot's still on. We might as well stir up the fire
and finish this meat," said Jim. He carved off a large chunk
of antelope with his butcher knife and took a bite. "This
roast is pretty good, boys."

"I doubt if he'll risk going into South Pass City, Jed.
He'll slip across the Sweetwater Plain and head for the
Popo Agie."

"If he knows the country, he will, Howie. I'll meet you
on the Seeds-kee-dee, two, three days I'd say," he nodded.

"That's a deal, hoss," smiled Jimmy.

The four men finished their meal and made preparations
for the chase. Jedediah, at a brisk trot, followed the four
sets of tracks heading north toward the Sweetwater. At the
same time, Charles, Jimmy and Howard relentlessly pursued
the ambushers across the desert, westbound. The trail was
easy to follow.

Ahead, Harry and the mules were half a mile in front of
Alfredo, Henry Lee and the corporal, who, all three afoot,
kept looking over their shoulders at the approaching dust trail.

"Riders behind us!" shouted the corporal. Henry Lee,
panic-stricken, ran frantically across the desert. "Dig you a
rifle pit, you fool," hollered the corporal, in vain.

Alfredo and the corporal dropped to their knees on the
desert floor and rapidly began scooping out shallow rifle
pits. From time to time Alfredo looked up at the ever
approaching riders. Out of the corner of his eye he saw
Henry Lee running and stumbling through the sagebrush.

Drawing closer to Alfredo and the corporal was Jimmy
on the big bay. At three hundred yards from the running
Henry Lee, Jimmy pulled his horse to a stop and dismounted,
falling prone, with his elbows dug into the sand. He ran
the rear sight to elevation and fired. The booming roar of
the heavy caliber Sharps seemed incongruous with the

stillness of the hot desert floor. Then all hell broke loose! The soft lead bullet caught Henry between the shoulder blades and blew out a chunk of shirt on his chest. For fifteen minutes Jimmy, Charles, and Howie exchanged shots across the sagebrush with Alfredo and the corporal. Harry's dust drifted with the wind three miles away. Alfredo and the corporal were good shots, but they were afoot and without water.

"What do you think?" wondered Charles.

"No gold; no water; no horses," said Jimmy.

They looked at each other and did not speak. Inching their way on their bellies, they retreated down the draw. In a crouch, they hurried along the arroyo to their mounts.

Meanwhile, miles to the west, Sampson slowed his string to let Harry catch up. "What happened?"

"Three riders. Henry's dead."

"Sixteen sacks of dust. Looking better all the time," they laughed.

"How far are they behind us?"

"Four or five miles. Your corporal slowed them down, lieutenant."

"I'll look him up if he makes it to San Francisco!" grinned Clark.

Long shadows cast by horse and rider ushered in a cooling evening breeze as the pair crossed the Oregon Trail and reached the Big Sandy River by dark.

The pursuers, Charles, Jimmy and Howard, now mounted, gave a wide berth to the expert riflemen and doggedly picked up the tracks of Harry and the lieutenant.

"We're closing, but I don't see them," Howie said with a slap to the top of his field glass case.

"Going to be hard to hide their trail. We might as well hole up for the night," said Jimmy.

"They're hightailing it out of here. Most likely ride all night," Charles said. He shifted his weight in the saddle. "We've both got water now. Should be a race."

As darkness approached they made bivouac preparations: picketed their stock, posted a watch, cooked their meal and spent a restless night while they discussed plans for the following day.

In the early dawn light there were no shadows. As soon as they could see the ground in front of them, they were on their way once more. At the Big Sandy, Jimmy held them up. "Tracks both up and down stream. They may have split up. Wait here while I have a look see."

Jimmy rode up the river about four-hundred yards and turned to repeat his search downstream. He dismounted for a closer look at the tracks and then afoot, led his horse back to his companions. "I don't know, Howard. They must have spent half the night riding up and down the river. Tracks everywhere. I lose them each way at about a hundred yards. Best to split up. You two go upstream; I'll go down."

Thirty miles north, the Big Sandy forms in the rugged Wind River Mountains. Thirty miles south, it joins the Green River at the Overland Stage Crossing. The Overland Trail, not to be confused with the Oregon Trail, was a route west that entered that country from Fort Collins on the Cache la Poudre River through Laramie City, Elk Mountain and Fort Halleck, down Pass Creek, through Bridger's Pass, LaClede Station on Bitter Creek and then across the Green River to Fort Bridger. It roughly paralleled the Oregon Trail, but was one-hundred miles south of that Trail. The sagebrush is taller over those hills, and the buffalo grass rich, but there are no trees. A horse and rider can be seen for miles.

The horse threw his ears forward at the sound of muffled gunshots coming from upriver. Jim turned him sharply and stared into the distance. With his glasses he could see for miles, but the mirage was his only reward. He kicked his horse to a lope. After three-quarters of a mile he stopped to listen. He heard several shots more clearly. He urged his horse on. He was out of the river and headed straight for the sound. Stopping again, he could see puffs of smoke, before he heard the sounds.

Somewhere ahead in the rolling foothills where deep gullies were cut by the meandering stream, Howard and Charles were caught in a crossfire and their two mules were dead. The lieutenant and Harry were lying in the rocks two hundred yards above them. They were using the dead mules as a breastwork while their horses ran at a full gallop down the stream bed. There went their transportation and survival.

Back down the escarpment, Jim pulled his horse to a stop within six hundred yards of the skirmish. He reached back and opened the flap to his saddlebag and removed his glasses. "They're both alive!" he said aloud. With a flip of the reins the horse bounded up the bank and out of the riverbed. Gunfire sounded down the slope as he worked his way through a draw and rode up a gentle slope to the same elevation as the ambushers. Tying his horse to a sagebrush, he pulled his Sharps from the scabbard, slung the Blakeslee cartridge box over his shoulder, unsheathed the Spencer repeater from the horn, and with a rifle in each hand, he slowly inched his way over the crest of the hill. Behind an outcrop of sandstone he took his stand. He removed his Hudson Bay blanket coat, folding it for a pad. He propped his cartridge box between a crevice in the stones and opened the lid. Looking over the situation below, Jimmy saw the outlaws' two horses and four mules tied above them in a sheltered depression. Howard and Charles could not see the mules, but the mules were four hundred yards away and slightly above Jimmy in the open.

Jimmy, still undetected, could not see the two men who

were pouring shots into the barricade of dead mules below. He could see shots coming up the hill from his partners, but they were wild and not effective.

Lowering the finger lever of the Sharps, Jimmy placed a linen cartridge in its breech and closed it. He pushed a cap on the nipple and laid it on the blanket. He tore the top off a box of Sharps cartridges and laid ten rounds on the rock. Using his field glasses, he could see a foot move behind the near mule and a shoulder behind the other mule. "They are still alive," he thought. He swung the glasses up the hill. Black-powder smoke billowed from behind the rocks; but still no target showed. "They won't last much longer," Jimmy thought.

He picked up the Sharps and centered the front shoulder of the farthest mule and fired. The mule dropped without a twitch as Jimmy reloaded and swung his sight onto the next mule. The thundering sound echoed above the heads of Harry and the lieutenant.

"The bastard is shooting the mules!" choked Harry from behind a large boulder.

The lieutenant rolled onto his back to look at the ridge above and to the north of them. "Where is he?" rasped Sampson.

Back up the ridge, Jimmy changed to the repeater and rapidly sailed seven shots around the rock below. He lifted his glasses for a closer look. "Howie? Howie? You all right?" he called. He saw movement below and repeated, "Charles, you all right?"

"Howard has been hit!"

"How bad?"

"In the arm."

"Can he move?"

"Yeah," hollered Howie, disgustedly.

"Move down the hill," ordered Jimmy. "If this pair wiggles, I'll blow 'em off the mountain!"

As they inched their way on their bellies, Jim fired rapidly at the rock, breaking off fragments and splattering gravel in a shower about the pair.

Safely below, in the stream bed, Howard and Charles worked their way out of rifle range. Their horses were out of sight, somewhere down the river.

The lieutenant tested Jim's intent by pushing a stick into the open above the large rock and moved it. It drew an immediate fusillade of accurate fire.

But this was a standoff. The lieutenant and Harry, entrenched behind a rock were safe from harm, while Howard was bleeding and without a horse.

Switching to the Sharps, Jim killed the other two mules and frightened the horses so badly that they pulled the sagebrush out of the ground, and in a frenzy, galloped up the hill.

He gathered his coat and rifles and in a run bounded into the saddle of his horse and shoved the Spencer home, but carried his Sharps. The horse ran at a full gallop down the hill and across the draw coming out at the river's edge. Jim trotted the pony to where Howard was sitting on the cutbank of the Sandy.

"How bad you hit?" asked Jimmy. "Can you ride?"

He shrugged his shoulders in pain, and lifted his blood soaked shirt away from the bullet hole. Charles had twisted his belt so tightly above Howard's wound that his hand was gray. In his haste to stop the flow of blood Charles had cut off all circulation to Howard's fingers.

"Let me have a look." Jim tore the shirtsleeve away and loosened the tourniquet. Color returned immediately. "Can you move your fingers?"

"I'm all right, Jim. Just a flesh wound," as he exercised his hand and arm for his friend.

"Not bleeding too badly. Missed the bone. You'll be good as new by first snow," smiled Jimmy.

"I'll go get your horses. They won't bother you," he nodded up the hill. "That gold isn't going anywhere. The mules are dead, and their horses are probably over in South Pass by now. You wait right here."

Two miles down the river the horses grazed along its bank. Jimmy caught them up and walked them back upstream. Upon reaching Howard, Jim said, "Straight east twenty miles to South Pass; then ruts of the Oregon Trail you can see in the dark. Eight or nine more miles to South Pass City," directed Jim. "Hell, only thirty miles. You'll be there in time for breakfast."

"I'll be back as soon as I can," promised Charles. "Now you stay sharp, hear?"

Jim went back to the same ridge to glass the countryside. He knew he wouldn't find the two outlaws who had ambushed Howard and Charles. The outlaws were taking advantage of the remaining daylight and were probably looking for their horses.

Jim tied his horse to some brush, sat on an outcrop and searched each draw for movement. Nothing. Not even a bird. He gathered his horse and rode down the slope. There was blood on the rock where the pair had lain. He circled looking for sign. They had returned to the dead mules but hadn't stayed long. He counted sixteen sacks of gold. There were no canteens, so they ought to have water. "Plenty of streams on this side of the divide." He looked up the hill, and walked his horse a short way looking for tracks. "They're up there," he thought. "Good place for an ambush." He chose to stay by the gold. It would take them two or three days to walk to South Pass City, longer if one of them was badly wounded. Charles will be back with pack animals before then.

He returned to Howie's dead mules and retrieved a few supplies. He cut the lash ropes and removed the upper packs. He unsuccessfully tried to free the packs on the downside. He found the coffee pot, skillet, bacon, flour, coffee and jerky. He recovered the extra ammunition for his Blakeslee tubes and a small sack of grain for his horse. Then he rode down hill for about two miles to discourage a night bushwhacking.

Deep in a sheltered crevasse, he lit a small fire for his supper and rolled out his blanket. At dark he grained his horse and tied him up short. "Last horse in these parts, I'm not going to take a chance," he thought. He kicked sand over the remaining coals of the campfire but saved one ember to light his pipe. He removed his boots, placed them under his saddle and then pulled the blanket up over his chest to ward off the cold desert evening. "Must be getting old," he thought. "I sure spend a lot of time thinking about that warm bed at Fort Laramie!"

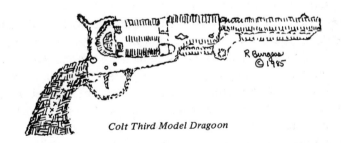

Colt Third Model Dragoon

CHAPTER TWENTY-FIVE

HOW'D YOU LIKE THAT?

The four sets of tracks were on a beeline course for the Sweetwater. "If they maintain this direction, they will cross it half way between South Pass City and Saint Mary's Stage Station," thought Jedediah.

At the same time, in the distance to the north, like an elk, watching his back trail, the outlaw stopped every twenty minutes to stare toward the wagon. He had no field glasses. Consequently, he looked for movement or dust. The woman made him nervous, but he gave her water. "You keep up, little lady, and you and me won't have no trouble!"

Amy took a long drink of water, spilling some of it down her front, then said, "Turn me loose. Please. I'll go into South Pass City and not tell a soul. I promise."

He grabbed the canteen from her hands and drank in long gulps with most of the water running down his neck and chest. He put the cork into the mouth of the canteen and drove it in with a hard blow from the heel of his hand and said, "You're coming with me, lady! You give me anymore sass and I'll tie your butt across that saddle and lash your feet and hands together under the belly of that horse. Now, how-would-you-like-that?" he said deliberately.

She dropped her eyes and shook her head no. For the first time, fright unnerved her, and a soft sob escaped her throat.

"From here on, I don't want to see you lagging behind. You keep that horse right alongside mine. You hear?"

"Yes," she answered softly.

They rode at a fast pace, rapidly leaving the desert. As they neared the Wind River Range, they kicked their horses constantly to keep them from pausing for a bunch of buffalo grass. Antelope grazed on almost every hillside, and deer were in several of the draws.

To the south, meanwhile, Jedediah knew that he couldn't cut the distance by maneuvering and that he wouldn't risk following their tracks. Instead, he made it up in speed. He swung to the left and headed toward South Pass and then turned right in a flanking movement. Pausing in a sheltered draw, Jed could see the outlaw and the girl. The outlaw was leading his mules at a walk. Jed urged his horse faster into a lope for two miles and then dismounted, jogged for two hundred yards, walked for fifty, climbed back in the saddle, and cantered for two more miles. He was making good time when he heard a shot.

At that moment, just south of the Sweetwater River, in the fading light the outlaw stopped his horse and killed a young buck deer. He cut out the chops along the backbone and packed them on the mule. Amy watched the man butcher the deer while she chanced long looks at their backtrail. She thought she saw movement down a long draw to the south. "If I only had field glasses," she thought. They crossed the Sweetwater and rode for another hour until they found a small stream with thick willows along its banks.

The night noises had increased, while the shadows

lengthened, as a lone figure hurried toward the changing colors of sunset. Jedediah had gotten above the outlaw and the girl when they stopped to butcher the deer. He waited for darkness. Along the creekbank the willows were thick, and in the dimness Jed watched the horses and mules of the pair as they stepped on fallen branches, breaking them with a crack that sounded like distant gunfire.

The noises of the broken branches intensified Amy's alertness, and she strained to get a glimpse of movement in the dusky willows south of the creek. His voice startled her. "You gather the wood and start the fire, woman, while I unpack these mules. No tricks." He turned to untie the lash ropes. Amy didn't answer, but started breaking dead willow branches to start a fire.

"I'm talking to you, woman. I expect to hear you answer back!"

"Very well. I'll start the fire and cook the meat." She didn't look up from her work at the creekbank.

"Now, answering me wasn't so hard was it?" he asked mockingly.

Again, Amy didn't speak, but continued to break willow branches into small pieces.

"I said, that wasn't so hard?" He spoke gruffly this time as he walked to her and grabbed her roughly and pulled her against him.

"No. That wasn't hard. Now please let me go. You're hurting me!" She brought both hands up against his chest and tried to break his grasp.

"It's getting dark and you ain't got much wood."

"Then I recommend that you help!"

"Ha! Howdy. I knew you could talk." He crudely pushed her away and turned to help her gather a pile of brush for their supper. She cut a skillet full of chops and fried them while the coffee boiled. Looking desperately toward the horses, she raced her mind wildly searching for a means of escape. One horse, picketed by a front foot, grazed along the creek. His halter was removed. The other horse grazed several yards down the creek. He likewise had no halter but was hobbled by the front feet.

Watching her every move as she leaned over the skillet and lifted the chops, he said, "You know, me and you could have us a time with all that gold. You'd like that?"

"Yes, I'd like that."

"Tell me how much you'd like that."

"I'd like that very much."

Pleased, he continued, "I aim to head to Montana." He grew more confident, "Buy me a claim. Or maybe a saloon. How'd you like that, little woman?" he asked with a thick voice.

"I think that would be fine." Her heart raced wildly as she tried to remain calm.

"I've got a bottle in my saddle bag. Get it!"

She did as she was told and handed it to him. He tipped it up and took a long drink. "Your turn." He handed her the bottle.

"No, thank you."

"Ah ha! You don't understand the rules. What I say, you do. Savvy?" He glared at her; his thick chest heaved while he waited for her answer.

"Yes."

"Your turn."

She took the bottle and tipped it to her lips, but didn't swallow much. She handed it back.

He took a long drink. "Turn around in the light," he ordered.

She didn't want to turn, felt the gooseflesh over her arms, but stepped near the fire. "I'm cold. May I get my jacket?"

"No. But you can have another drink." He shoved the bottle into her face.

168

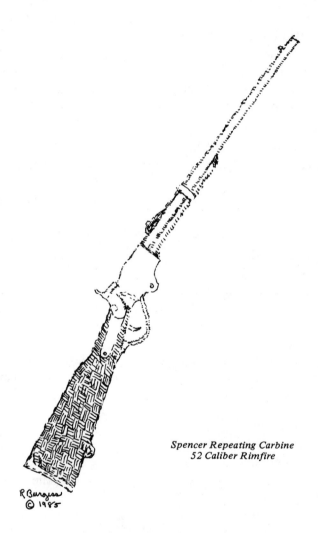

Spencer Repeating Carbine
52 Caliber Rimfire

R Burgess
© 1985

She tipped the bottle and drank, choking slightly on the raw hot liquid.

"Now!" he demanded. "Unbutton that purdy shirt! Turn to the light where I can see."

She slowly turned toward the light and unbuttoned the top three buttons and stopped.

"Now lean over that fire again." He saw her, petrified, long black hair silhouetted against the firelight. "Move!" he almost whispered.

He stepped behind her and ran his hand over her breasts and down her back to her buttocks, then inside her thighs. "Now. I want you to remove that garter gun and do it real slow. Savvy?"

The color had left her face, and she was not sure what she should do. She felt stark fear for the first time. "You got it out real quick before, didn't you, little woman? Huh?" he grunted.

"Yes."

"Now, unbutton that skirt with your right hand. All them buttons. Purdy. Now with your left hand. Slowly. Pull that pistol and drop it where I can see it."

Just at this moment of distracted concentration, Jedediah stepped into the firelight with his sawed-off shotgun cradled over his left arm. The outlaw was dumbfounded. He couldn't believe another soul was on this mountain. He squinted through the brightness of the campfire, tried to recognize the stranger who stood with legs slightly spread apart holding a short barreled shotgun with both hammers dogged back. The outlaw went for his gun. The explosion was deafening!

After a few seconds the echo of the blast died out down the canyon and in the silence Amy shook with an uncontrollable rage and deep, racking sobs.

Jedediah, his eyes narrowed, looked at the woman while walking to the dead man. Upon crossing the firelight he turned the man over with his foot. Satisfied that he was no longer a threat, he turned to the woman. "I've been following you for hours, Miss Stafford. My name's Jedediah Caldwell. Howard asked me to help you."

She continued to shake and couldn't speak. Jed walked near her and said, "You're just tired and cold, Miss. A little coffee and a warm blanket and you'll feel better."

She couldn't control the spasms that clutched at her throat. Jedediah wrapped her in two blankets and built up a huge fire. He gave her coffee until she calmed down, some thirty minutes later.

"My God, I haven't cried like that in twenty years!"

"Well, you're gonna have to take to wearing your pistol on the outside, Miss!"

They laughed hysterically until tears came to their eyes. Slowly Amy regained her composure while Jedediah made his bed across the fire from her, all the while keeping up a steady stream of conversation about Howard, Jimmy and Charles and their preparation and adventures pursuing her captors across the desert. He looked up from his pipe; she was sound asleep. He crossed to her bed, gently pulled the blanket up under her chin and noted for the first time the pleasing appeal of her sunburned face. "Howard's a lucky man," he thought.

Jedediah returned to his bed and went to sleep just before the fire went out.

Several hours later, Jedediah awakened with a start. A Canada Jay, wings aflutter, landed near the cold campfire and pecked at scraps left from the night before. He looked across at the girl, curled in a ball with the wool blanket pulled up over her head. He watched her sleep for a few minutes and saw the blanket move and she looked intently at him. "I guess we were both a little tired," Jedediah said. He threw back his blanket and added small twigs to the cold bed of ashes. "You hungry?" He didn't wait for an answer. He struck a match on a rock with his right hand and stuck it under the small pile of tinder while adding slivers of wood with his left hand. It burst into flame.

"There," he said, satisfied. "Coffee in a few minutes. Elk along the stream. Been watching us for thirty minutes. Gonna be a fine day."

"You never told me your name."

He grinned. "She must not have heard a word I said last night," he thought.

"Jedediah, Ma'am. Jedediah Caldwell. Look at that. Elk right in with our horses. Plenty of grass and good water. Those horses won't want to leave. If I was a horse, I wouldn't mind staying right here. Over on the Popo Agie the grass is even deeper. And mountain sheep. Thick as sagebrush. They'll eat right out of your hand. Winters are warm in the valley."

"Where do you winter, Mr. Caldwell?"

"Oh," he thought for a moment, "South. Santa Fe. Maybe Taos. Spent the whole winter in Mexico several years ago. Didn't like it, though. Down there, you can't get away from the desert. Up here you can go around it." He pulled on his boots. "Unless you're looking for gold and a pretty woman," he smiled softly at her. Then embarrassed, "My goodness, I've been talking so much; but then I haven't had much chance to visit with a lady," he blushed.

They finished breakfast and caught the horses. The mules were sound and looked in good shape. The horses, on the other hand, were thin and had several cuts. The fetlock of one was badly swollen. The other had thrown a shoe.

"Well, at least we can make it to South Pass City."

Amy looked up with a start. "I can't go there!"

"Ma'am?"

"I mean . . . It's just . . . Isn't there someplace closer?"

"It's only fifteen miles."

"How far is it to railhead?"

"Hundred miles."

"Fort Bridger?"

"We have to go through South Pass City to get to Fort Bridger. I have to trade some of these animals and buy some more mules. My partners are somewhere south of here. They'll be needing supplies soon."

"Is Mr. Prescott with them?"

"Yes, ma'am."

"Did he go after the others?"

"Three of them left the same time I did. Should have caught up with them by now."

"Did they take the gold with them?"

"Strange sight. Thought more of the gold than they did of their lives. All those horses, and they were walking!"

"Wouldn't you have done that?"

"No, ma'am. I'd have buried the stuff and rode out. Been in the ground for thousands of years, a little more time won't hurt."

"Are you going to bury this gold?" she asked, pointing toward the panniers that the outlaw had brought with them.

"No, ma'am. This is Howie's gold."

"Mr. Prescott doesn't own the gold; he was just freighting it," she reminded him.

"He loses it; he owns it, Miss Stafford."

"May I see what a sack of gold dust looks like, Mr. Caldwell?"

"Sure," he said. He unbuckled the canvas flap of the aparejos and untied the heavy canvas bag. He pulled the edge of the sack down to the top of the gold and stepped back.

"It's lovely," she beamed, plunging her hand into the sack. The fine gold dust stuck to her hands and glittered softly. "How much is here?"

"Forty pounds."

"No. I mean how much is all this worth? Both packsacks full?"

"Sixty to seventy thousand dollars."

"I can see now why Mr. Prescott is trying so hard to get it back."

"And why that lieutenant and his bunch is trying so hard to take it," Jedediah added.

"Why are you here, Jedediah?"

"Howard's a friend of mine." She looked at him and didn't say anything. She waited expectantly. "I was a scout for the cavalry on the Powder River," he continued. "Major Prescott was my commanding officer. We rode a lot of trails together. Fort Reno, Fort Phil Kearny, and Fort Laramie. We're friends."

"He's going to pay you, isn't he?"

"We didn't discuss it."

A brief flash of anger crossed her face. "You didn't discuss it? Risking your life in this God-awful desert and you didn't discuss it?"

"I came after you, Miss Stafford. I never met you. Howard's a friend of mine," he repeated, coldly.

"I'm sorry. Jedediah, I'm sorry."

He picked up his saddle and roughly threw it on his horse. In silence he quickly packed the mules and saddled Amy's horse. He had become angry and wasn't sure why.

"Now, what's this about South Pass?"

She didn't know what to tell him. She couldn't tell him the truth. She liked Howard, but not enough to marry him. That lady at the hotel had seen her with Harry and was suspicious from the first. She's probably Howard's lover. It's his stage stop. His bed. She probably keeps it warm for him. Then there's the lieutenant; she could never tell him about their relationship.

"Jedediah," she pleaded, with her dark eyes sparkling, and a mischievous flick of her tongue over her lips, "I don't want to go into that town."

He didn't know what to make of her. Mysterious, forthright, with a sensuousness that could render a man helpless. He looked straight into her eyes. "I'll figure something out," he said. "I've got to get more horses."

She smiled her thanks and bounced onto her horse.

"Hey!" he said. She stopped with one hand on the horn of her saddle. "What did you do with that tiny gun?" he asked.

Amy blushed, broke out in a wide grin, and then patted her blouse between her breasts.

Jedediah shook his head, speechless.

By noon they were on Willow Creek approaching South Pass City from below.

"I'll be back before dark. You ever use one of these things?" Jedediah asked. He pulled his Henry rifle from its scabbard.

"No."

"Nothing to it." He levered a round into the chamber. "It's loaded and cocked. When you pull the trigger, you jack another round into the chamber, and it stays cocked and ready to fire."

He let the hammer down. "You try it. Don't pull the trigger. You'll have every miner on the mountain down here!"

She went through the cycle to his satisfaction and then he turned to the mules and slipped their packs. "I'll trade these animals. Howie has a whole corral full of stock up there. You need anything?"

"Well, I haven't had a bath in days; I've lost all my clothes and my hair looks like that horse's tail, but other than that I don't need anything!" Amy said with a grin that made him want to melt.

He looked at her dirty riding skirt and her floppy hat framing her charcoal smudged face and said, "We can both use a bar of soap." He reached for the rifle she held and touched her hand, unintentionally. For an instant their eyes met. He tried to look away, but couldn't. A crimson flush began at his neck, spread upward to his face and shone through his dark, suntanned skin. Speechless, he turned, laid the Henry on a pack and mounted his horse. "Damn, what a woman," he thought. He rode up Willow Creek into town, unable to get her out of his mind.

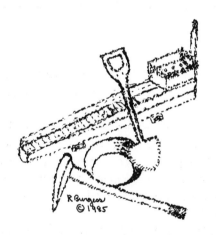

CHAPTER TWENTY-SIX

YOU A MINER?

The blacksmith at the Black Horse Livery told him to turn his mules into the pasture and take whatever stock and tack he needed. "I heard about the holdup. Everyone in town knows about it by now," said the blacksmith. "Killed old Pervins. Drove stages all his life. I hope they don't hurt that little lady. She kind of gave a lift to this town while she was here." He bent over and picked up a piece of chain from the floor and laid it over the anvil and then turned to Jedediah. "Is Mr. Prescott all right?"

"He's just fine. I expect to join him tomorrow, and that little lady is south of town waiting for me to trade these mules."

The blacksmith grinned and then said, "Come on, I'll help you saddle your stock."

They cut four fresh mules and two strong horses from the herd and haltered them. Jed saddled his mount. He outfitted two mules with packsaddles and panniers; the other two with sawbucks only. Jed and the blacksmith spent an hour at this work. He tailed the string and led them across the log bridge spanning Willow Creek and around the corner to the long, low general store across the street from the Prescott Hotel. Several freight wagons crowded the street.

There weren't many goods in the general store, but there were necessities enough to get them over South Pass: a slab of bacon and a sack of flour, a sack of coffee and some dried apples and sugar, a can of baking powder and salt, a forty-two round box of Spencer cartridges for Jimmy and a hundred rounds of .44 rimfire, several sacks of dried vegetables, a small mirror and a bottle of whiskey. He held up several shirts and laid them down.

"Too small for you, mister."

"Not for me. For just a little thing. About this high," he measured to his chest.

"A boy?"

"No. A woman."

"Run her in here; maybe we can fit her."

"She's not here. She's south of here."

"You a miner?"

"Nope."

"Give me these two shirts and this pair of breeches. And a comb. A half a dozen of these bandanas. And a bar of soap."

The clerk watched him pick through the meager supplies. "Two hundred pounds of grain." Jedediah looked up and down the shelves.

"Anything else?"

"A couple of foot of that red ribbon," Jedediah pointed and noticed the clerk with a teasing grin on his face. Embarrassed, he stammered, "For her hair." Jed walked back to the counter and said, "Charge it to Howard Prescott. All except the ribbon. I'll pay for that."

A woman in the corner looked up from her shopping to say, "Do you know Mr. Prescott?"

"Yes, ma'am."

"Do you know where he is?"

"South of here."

"My name is Lillian Montgomery. I manage the Prescott Hotel. Could we talk in my office?"

"Jedediah Caldwell, ma'am. I'm pleased to meet you."

Jedediah followed her across the street. She maintained a very business-like manner. "She is well dressed and a little younger than me, and while not beautiful, she is attractive," he thought.

"Mr. Caldwell, I was very uneasy about that gold shipment and I told Howard so, but he insisted on getting it through. Have you recovered any of it?"

"No, ma'am. Not exactly. Not yet."

"Is Howard all right?"

"He was the last time I saw him."

"When was that?"

"Two days ago."

"Is he alone?"

"No. Jimmy Robineaux and Charles Richfield are with him. Both are good men. Now, Miss Montgomery, don't you worry about Howie. He can take care of himself."

"How about the girl?"

"She's all right."

"Is she with Howard?"

"No. Not right this minute."

"Mr. Caldwell, I don't believe you are telling me everything."

"I kind of have that feeling too, Miss Montgomery," Jedediah said.

"I'm worried about Howard. I don't think that girl wants to marry him. She seemed very friendly with a man here in town for a week before their trip south. They left on the stage together."

"What do you know about this fellow?"

"All I know is that he came down from Montana. People

called him 'Harry'. He seemed to have plenty of money. I think he knew about the gold on the freight wagon. He spent two or three weeks here in town. I don't think he did anything except drink and gamble."

"It looks like he had plenty of company, doesn't it, ma'am? I'll tell Howie you're well," Jedediah said politely.

He walked back across the street to the general store where the proprietor told him, "I took the liberty of packing your goods into your panniers, mister. All they need is your lash rope."

"Much obliged, friend," Jedediah said. He took the ropes off the sawbuck and tied his diamond over each load.

Meanwhile down Willow Creek Amy grew restless and very lonely, but her spirits lifted when she saw the packstring winding through the brush.

"You look happy," he grinned.

"It's lonely around all that gold," Amy said.

Stepping down to the ground from his saddle, Jed tied his horse to a willow branch and secured the mules.

Amy sensed his aloofness as she watched him saddle her horse. He packed the gold onto the two mules and did not speak while loading the gold, but when he finished he said, "You should get on that horse and ride straight to the hotel. Take the next stage to California!" He wasn't looking at her. He was afraid to. She didn't answer him. He continued, "You have no business out here. This is no place for a woman. You should be home in New Orleans." His voice grew louder as he talked.

"Here's your rifle, Jedediah," she said softly.

He took it from her and stuck it into the boot under the stirrup. He fussed with the strap on his saddlebag and then glanced at her. She looked as if she was going to cry.

"Do you know what you are doing? You have almost been killed!" He was nearly shouting.

"I want to go with you, Jedediah," she said in a soft
quivering voice.

He took a deep breath and had difficulty controlling the
urge to crush her in his arms. "God knows where we are
heading. Probably run out of water. You shouldn't be here!"

He pushed his horse over with his shoulder and then raised
her horse's right front foot by the fetlock to inspect the shoe.

"Four hours of daylight. We might as well get a couple
of miles down the trail."

Six miles below the town they reached the Sweetwater
and stopped to make camp for the night. There was a thicket
of willow trees for shelter with the riverbank at their feet.
The day's heat still lingered, but it would be cold in another
hour. A roaring fire, quickly kindled from dry brush, heated
the evening coffee.

"I brought you a change of clothing. There's a mirror,
comb and soap in the sack. Help yourself."

She took her blanket and the sack and went to the river.
She made no attempt to hide her nakedness from him as she
was aware of his wish to honor her privacy. She washed her
hair and scrubbed her skin pink. The evening air was cold as
she dried quickly and wrapped the blanket around her
shoulders. She went to the fire for warmth.

"Coffee's on."

"I feel so good. That's the first bath I've had in days.
And my hair!"

"Is the water cold?" He didn't wait for her answer but
continued stirring water into a pan of flour for bannock.
"I've got the bacon sliced and the dried vegetables are
soaking. You want to start supper while I scrub off some of
this sand?" he said.

"Sure, but you'd better hurry. The sun is going down and
it's getting cold."

She combed her hair and smiled, pleased at the sight of
the red ribbon, laid neatly on top of her new shirt. Her face

glowed with warmth from the fire. The soft flannel shirt hung loosely, a little too big, but it was comfortable. It brought back memories of her childhood, reminded her of pleasant afternoons in New Orleans when she used to try on her mother's gowns and pretend. Her thoughts turned to San Francisco and Sacramento and the beautiful wardrobe she had brought with her that was now strewn about the desert. She glanced toward the river where the big man splashed while he swam. Such a wild man. "He's lived out here fifteen years," she thought. "He loves it. He's like a child. He's such a gentle man. Oh, my God, Amy," she thought, "get a hold of yourself or you'll fall in love with this mountain man!"

She set the coffee pot to the back of the fire and reached for two plates. "You hungry?" she asked, as he returned from the river.

"Like I've never been before," Jedediah said. He dried his hair and combed it straight back. And then he noticed the red ribbon in her still-wet, dark black hair.

"Thick soup. It will warm you up," she said. She handed him a plate. "It's cold on this pass."

"What's it like in New Orleans?" he questioned, looking at her intently.

"There are many people. And a lot more water than here. And even in the middle of winter it's not as cold as the water in that river." She laughed, her eyes sparkling.

"This is good soup, Amy. And hot."

"Food is one thing we're noted for in New Orleans. Spain and France left their influence on our culture, especially our cooking. Of course, we eat a lot of seafood. We don't have big game like you do out here. I enjoy buffalo steak. My favorite, though, is loin steak of the antelope with sourdough biscuits and milk gravy. I have to watch what I eat, I gain weight so easily."

Jedediah looked at her trim figure; she couldn't weigh

more than one hundred twenty pounds. Amy saw his appraising look and blushed. The willow branches crackled with a hot fire as he built it up for the night. He spread their beds on each side of the flame and covered Amy with an extra blanket.

"There," he said. "Are you warm?"

"No."

He didn't know what to say, so turned back to the fire and threw on some more wood. "I'll mix you a hot toddy, if you'd like."

"That does sound good, Jedediah."

He put a pan of water over the fire to heat for the toddy, rinsed out their cups, added sugar to the bottom, walked to his saddlebag for the whiskey and poured a generous amount into the cup. He reached for the hot water, adding it to the mixture and stirred the contents of each cup. "Don't have any spices. Haven't seen a lemon in twenty years. But this will warm you." He handed Amy the cup.

They enjoyed the toddy and reminisced of the past. The fire began to die down and in the stillness he heard her say, "Jedediah."

He did not answer.

"Jedediah, I'm cold." There was a long pause.

"I'm cold, Jedediah."

CHAPTER TWENTY-SEVEN

DON'T LEAVE ME LIKE THIS!

The horses had run at full speed for three-quarters of a mile, stopped and turned to look downhill toward the sound of gunfire. They commenced to graze, drifting slowly toward the pass.

Sampson had spotted the horses early that morning. "I'll catch them, Harry. You stay here."

Harry had lost a lot of blood from a wound that had exposed his jawbone. A shirttail bandage, tied over the top of his head, made it difficult for him to keep his hat on in the wind.

The lieutenant walked slowly toward the horses. They threw up their heads at the sound of him coming. They walked away, nervously dropping their heads to pull up large tuffs of buffalo grass. "Whoa, boy," he soothed. Each time he approached them, they trotted off a shorter distance until they finally ignored him. Then he grabbed their reins.

Having lost all their accoutrements except what they had

carried with them, the lieutenant and Harry rode straight
for South Pass City, stopping first at the livery.

"I need six mules and two fresh horses," Clark said.

"Ain't got much left," said the blacksmith, with a wave
of the hand. "Most of 'em are lame. This country is sure
hell on horses." And with that, he turned back to his forge.

Harry and the lieutenant, discouraged with the blacksmith's
lack of interest in their problem regarding their need for
fresh horses and mules, stomped across the corral mumbling
insults about the blacksmith's character. Crossing the
footbridge over Willow Creek, they entered the back door
of the Willow Bend Saloon.

"You got any bandages?" inquired the lieutenant.

"Over at the drugstore," nodded the bartender, "across
the street."

Harry found a table in the corner and ordered a whiskey.
"Leave it," he motioned to the bartender with the long
side burns and bald head.

At the same time Clark crossed the wide dirt street and up
the steps to the door of the drugstore. A young clerk was the
only other person in the building.

"I need some bandages and something to clean a wound."

"What kind of wound?"

"Bullet. Across the face." He pointed to his jaw.

The clerk went to a shelf and took down some supplies.
"That be all?" he asked while he poured some powder into
a bottle. He added water from a stoppered bottle and shook
the concoction vigorously.

"Yes."

"Five dollars."

Clark Sampson paid the man, picked up the bottle of
medicine, turned to the door and hastily strode across
the street. He entered the front door of the saloon. He
walked to the corner table where Harry downed his third
shot-glass of whiskey. Sampson uncorked the medicine

bottle, emptied some of the contents onto a cloth bandage and applied it immediately to Harry's wound.

"What the hell is in that stuff?" grimaced Harry.

"Some kind of acid. Carbolic or something. The druggist said it should make the wound heal."

"There won't be anything left to heal!" cracked Harry, as he tipped the whiskey bottle up and downed a healthy slug.

"The laceration is not as bad as it looked at first. It will heal in a few days, but you better stay here and change the dressing."

"I'm going with you," responded Harry.

"Suit yourself. We'll need a couple of men until we get those sacks on our packmules." They looked around the room for prospective back-shooters. This saloon was full of them. They picked two.

"Five hundred dollars apiece. That's the deal. One hundred now," he counted. "The rest when we get our goods."

"Where'd you say you lost your supplies?" asked a tall miner.

"I didn't."

"What we supposed to do for that five hundred dollars?" inquired the miner's drinking partner.

"We were ambushed by road agents. They killed our mules. We came here for a string and some guns." The lieutenant looked at the pair and narrowed his eyes. "We've found the mules; with you two helping us we've got the guns!"

"How many men guarding your goods, soldier boy?" asked the miner, talking deliberately with his mouth full of food, while he sopped a chunk of bread in a plate of beans.

"One, maybe two. We hit one of them. He won't give us any trouble."

"What you got on that string that's worth fightin' fer?" wondered the man called Jake. He talked rapidly. "You must have some valuable property."

"Our winter supplies. We've got a claim over on Meadow Gulch."

"Hell, man, you can buy everything in that store across the street for two thousand dollars. You take us fer fools?" Jake sneered, with the corner of his mouth twitching, while his bushy, dark eyebrows formed a triangle following the wrinkles of his forehead.

The lieutenant, realizing he wasn't getting anywhere, changed his story. "Okay, it's sacks of dust. We're leaving our diggin's. We aim to take what's ours." He wasn't sure he convinced them, but he said it loudly and firmly.

"One thousand apiece. And five hundred now," demanded the miner.

"Done," said the lieutenant. "Meet us at the livery in an hour."

While packing their provisions on two mules, Harry said, "I'll shoot that tall bastard, first chance I get!" Hearing hollow clunking sounds on the bridge, he looked toward the riders. "Here they come now. Look at those sorry fleabags they're riding. You sure we want to take this pair with us?"

"Howdy, lieutenant," Jake said. "Looks like you got them mules ready to go."

"They're ready. I'm not sure you two are though, by the looks of your horses. Is this the best you can do?" Sampson asked, pointing at their mounts. "Where's your canteen?"

"We thought you'd have all the gear, soldier," said the tall man. "That's what you've trained for all your life, ain't it?"

The lieutenant didn't speak, but turned, disgusted to the mules and fetched two extra canteens and threw one to each of the backshooters. "Let's get down the trail."

After riding for more than two hours in the gathering of long shadows at their backs, Jake grumbled, "Where's it at?"

"Another five miles. We'll camp here and wait for morning," answered Sampson.

"Let's take 'em this evening and be back in town by midnight," suggested the tall man, confidently.

"There's an ole boy watchin' us right now," Harry said. "He might have something to say about that."

"Where?" Jake blurted.

"He's out there. Shoots a buffalo rifle. Killed our mules with one shot apiece. Good four hundred yards. All hit at the same spot through the shoulder."

"Jake licked his lips. "Got a drink?"

"Not until we've finished," promised Sampson. "You boys didn't even bring water, remember?"

"I'll go check the mules with my glasses," stated Harry. "Be back at dark."

The strong sage smell mixed with alkali dust was tinged with the putrid stench of rotting flesh. Harry continued his downwind approach and noticed large black ravens bunched along a bare ridge. From time to time, one sailed gracefully to the depression and with a flutter of wings, landed amid the carcasses. Harry still could not see the animals. He left his horse and afoot proceeded, bent at the waist, to edge closer for a better look.

In just one day the wolves had stripped every particle of hide and flesh from the bones of each mule. In a pile, the brownish contents of partially digested grass marked the spot where they had consumed the viscera. The pack saddles were in shreds, and the gold sacks damaged, but a little shovel work would fix that. Harry dropped to his knees and examined the sacks. The sight of the yellow metal took his breath away. "All mine!" he said aloud.

From behind a sandstone outcrop a dark shadow appeared, like an apparition. "You like this gold so much, pard, I'll let you watch it all night," pledged Jimmy, talking softly, as he cocked the hammer on his Sharps. In the fading light the soft, but unmistakable metallic sound of the sear engaging the tumbler was deafening.

Drawing back in abject terror, Harry begged, "I'll split it with you!" The dimness of Harry's face darkened the contours at the corner of his mouth while his eyes silently pleaded for mercy.

"You haven't got anything to split, pilgrim," said Jimmy, talking while he bit off a large hunk of twisted tobacco leaf.

"Look, I've got enough gold up in Montana to set you up for life," implored Harry. "You can have any part of it you want!"

"Why don't you just tell me where it is, and we can pay the army for the troopers you killed? And maybe for Mr. Prescott's horses and mules, not to mention the bullet he took."

Harry, still on the ground, drew away from Jimmy. "What are you doing?" he demanded in a shrill voice.

Jimmy pushed the man against a rock and threw a length of rawhide to him. "Tiing your feet." The scout slipped a length of aspen branch behind Harry's knees and forced him to sit up while bringing his flexed elbows up tight against the aspen pole thus squeezing it tighter against his knees. Jimmy tied Harry's wrists together in front of his shins and knotted the rope securely to the pole.

"My God, man, don't leave me like this! I don't have a chance. I can't move."

"More chance than that Gatling gun gave them drivers and them soldiers."

"I didn't do that!" screeched Harry; "it was the corporal!"

"You just came along for the gold," added Jimmy, drily. "Wolves won't bother a man who's moving. Indians will. I wouldn't make much noise tonight." He paused, barely able to see Harry in the darkness. "How many men with you?" he asked softly.

"Three. Three. God damit! I'll tell you anything!"

"Where they camped?"

"Five miles."

"What about the girl?"

"She was going to marry Prescott. I swear! I met her in New Orleans. We had some fun. That's all. We had a drink in South Pass. Old times."

"The lieutenant?"

"He set the whole thing up. Wired me in Virginia City. Told me I could make more money on one job than I'd make in a year in Montana."

"How did you know there was gold on the wagon?"

"You kidding? Everyone in town knows when gold leaves the Sweetwater." He struggled in his bonds, but could hardly move. "Cut me loose!"

"I'll let your friends do that."

Without a backward glance Jimmy faded into the darkness and retrieved Harry's horse. He could hear the night noises in the early dusk here on the Sandy.

Meanwhile, to the east, the tall miner and Jake were getting restless. Jake was having second thoughts about this job and needed a drink. "Where's your partner?" asked the miner.

"Didn't hear no shots," said Jake.

"Think he's carting off all that gold?" queried the miner.

The lieutenant had been thinking just that. He couldn't carry more than two sacks. Hell, he wants more than that. Probably stayed to fondle every damn sack.

"He'll show up directly," assured Sampson.

"One less man. Me and Jake gonna have to have more money," reasoned the tall man. He looked at the lieutenant expectantly.

Coyotes could be heard all up and down the divide. "Something's sure dead tonight, boys," said the lieutenant. "What's your price?"

"Five thousand apiece," said the miner. Jake nodded agreement and licked his lips.

"I'll have to pay you in dust after we get it."

"That will be just dandy," said the tall man, smiling at Jake.

CHAPTER TWENTY-EIGHT

BUSHWHACKER!

"Those lights sure look good, Charles. My arm feels like it's going to fall off," Howard told him.

"Better loosen that strap, Howie."

The tie rails along the street were full tonight. They could hear rapid runs on a banjo, the happy sounds of a man who loved his music; guitars played the melody, sweet-sad songs of lonely men and lonelier women; laughter, high pitched, low, gutteral, tinkling laughter; whiskey sounds of the night coming from several buildings. There was a coal-oil lamp at the desk of the Prescott Hotel, its wick needed trimming and it gave out very little light, but no attendant was present.

"Top of the stairs," Howie said.

Charles tapped on the door, "Miss Montgomery?"

"Who is it?"

"Howard's been hurt."

Down the hallway a door opened, a woman's face appeared and quickly the door closed. He could hear muffled voices coming from other rooms along the narrow corridor.

"Bring him in. Oh, Howard! That gold is not worth it! How bad are you hurt? Here on my bed."

Howard sat on the edge of the bed and the two of them helped him off with his boots.

"I'll go get Doc Jackson and some bandages," Lillian said. Worried, she picked up a shawl and draped it around her shoulders and hurried out the door.

"Is he a good doctor, Howie?"

"He owns the drug store. He does what he has to do."

Charles started a fire in the cast iron stove and filled a kettle with water. "You'll be fixed up in no time," Charles said reassuringly.

Shortly Lillian reappeared with Doc Jackson, a short man with dark trousers, half unbuttoned shirt and no coat. He peered intently at the arm. "Nasty wound, Howard. It should clean up though. You lost more blood than you should have. Ought to know better. Should have stopped and propped that arm up in the air!" He looked sternly at Howard.

"Hell, doc, a coyote would have chewed it off where we were at," laughed Howie.

Lillian filled a wooden tub with hot water and tested it with her hand. She appeared disgusted.

"What's that for?" Howie asked suspiciously.

"I'm going to give you a bath. You smell like the livery barn!" Lillian said. "You may have had a packtrain full of supplies, but it's obvious that you didn't have a bar of soap. Now, get in that tub!"

"I'll go take care of the horses, Howie," Charles said hastily. "Then I'll see if I can't find me a bath down the street. I need a change of clothes, too," Charles said. "I'll see you in the morning."

"Well? What are you waiting for! I've seen you naked before. Get in that tub!" Lillian repeated.

"Looks like you can handle the rest of it, Miss

Montgomery. Keep that dressing dry. I'll be over in the morning to change it. Good night, Howie."

"Thanks, doc. I appreciate it," Howard said sincerely.

Howard stood and fumbled with his shirt with his one good hand. He was all thumbs.

"Here, I'll do that," Lillian said tenderly.

In the street, Charles walked toward the dance hall which had the rooms for the girls upstairs. He squeezed into the crowded room. "You wanna dance?" came from a tiny thing with ruby-red lips.

"I want a bath," Charles answered.

"Upstairs, sweety," she smiled.

At the top of the stairs he met a richly dressed middle-aged woman who said, "I'm Belle. I run this place."

"I'm Charles, and I need a bath, a change of clothes, a cigar and whiskey," he grinned. "For starters!" he added.

"Girls, take care of Mr. Charlie's needs," she smiled.

At the end of the hall, in a small room a buxom, scantily-clad redhead stood by a deep wooden tub filled with hot water. "You like it hot?" she asked, emptying boiling water from the big vessel.

"Yea," he gulped.

She put the kettle back onto the stove.

"Whiskey?"

"Please."

She poured him a water glass half-full of whiskey and handed it to him. "Cigar?"

"Um huh."

She untied the front of her gown and let it drop to the floor. She smiled at Charles and bent over for a bar of soap. He watched her step into the tub and sit down.

"Get in," she said. "I'll scrub your back."

The following morning, Howard had breakfast in bed after Lillian shaved him.

Across the street Charles had a big breakfast down in the
kitchen. These were the first eggs he had seen since leaving
Omaha. All this grub freighted up from End of Track was
a welcome luxury. Hot biscuits and jam, buffalo steak and
gravy with lots of coffee. Finishing breakfast, Charles walked
out the door and up the stairs to Miss Montgomery's room.
"You get plenty of rest now, Howie."

"I hate to ask you to do this, Charles. I should be out
there. I feel so bad about this wound."

"Look at that hand. Swollen up like a tick. You mind
what Miss Lillian says, and you'll be as good as new when I
get back."

"There are some good men here, Charles. I can recruit
you some help."

"Won't be necessary. Jim will be looking for me. I can
make better time by myself. I'd waste a whole day here
trying to outfit someone else."

"You're probably right, Charles. But I feel so damn bad
about not being able to go with you!"

"I understand. I better be going if I'm going to find Jim
by dark."

"Good luck, Charles, and thanks!"

He had his packhorse loaded light with no more than
grain, food and canteens. He could make faster time with
two horses and would have a spare riding horse. Sunlight
brightened the upper slopes around the town, but around
Willow Creek it was still dark and damp with a pocket of
heavy fog layered along its upper reaches. Riding through
the mist he suddenly came out into the bright sunlight. It
was still early morning when he descended to the headwaters
of the Sandy and stopped to glass ahead. He could see
ravens circling, miles below in the rolling foothills. He
continued at a trot on down the stream.

On the west side of South Pass, the sun was higher, and
Jimmy knew they would be coming out of the east. "They

won't circle. They'll stay to the east and keep the sun to their backs," he thought.

At the same time the lieutenant stopped a mile above the mules and waited for the sun to climb a few more degrees. "He's tied to a stake. Right in front of the gold," reported Sampson.

"See anybody else?" asked Jake.

"No."

"What will we do?" Jake wondered.

"Let's get a little closer," Sampson said. Walking, he led his horse and in a single file, they stopped six hundred yards above Harry. "He's moving!" Sampson whispered.

Coyotes sat on high mounds around the area, but several hundred yards away. The men watched the hills for an hour. Ravens cleaned up small pieces that had been dragged to remote spots away from the site.

"You stay here with the horses, Jake. We'll go down for a look. We'll wave you in if it looks all right," said the lieutenant.

They cautiously worked their way to within fifty yards. The only movement below was the torn ends of Harry's shirtsleeve flapping in the breeze.

"Go down and untie him," Sampson ordered.

"I'm not going anywhere until we find who tied him up," said the miner. "Who you got chasing you out here?"

Cocking the hammer of his .44 Remington, Sampson put the muzzle in the miner's ear and said, "You think I'm going to pay you five thousand dollars just to ride thirty miles? Now get moving!"

The tall miner almost ran the fifty yards and quickly cut Harry's bonds.

"Water. Please!" Harry choked. He couldn't stand. He couldn't walk. His circulation started to improve as he exercised his extremities, but he could not walk. "That son of a bitch!" Harry spat.

Sharps Model 1852
52 Caliber

R Burgess
© 1985

Back up the hill, Jake held the horses and watched the
activity below him. Caught up in the drama being played
out around the dead mules, he didn't see the silent figure
twenty feet from him.

"Bushwhacker!" said the voice in a low firm tone.

Jake dropped the lead ropes of the horses and whirled
to face the challenger. He saw a muscular, dark skinned,
black haired man dressed in a blanket coat holding a belt
axe. Jake looked at the axe and then at the man; and drew!
The axe turned over once as it buried in his chest. The horses
trotted off several yards. Jimmy retrieved his axe, wiped it
in the grass, and stuck it in his belt. He turned and trotted
through the sagebrush, picking up two horses as he went.

"The mules are getting away," yelled the miner, as he
raised his rifle.

"Don't shoot! You'll frighten them." He had his glasses
out looking for Jake. "Do you see anything?"

"No," said the miner.

"Where's Jake?" Sampson asked, alertly searching the
hill above.

"I don't see him."

"Let's get up there."

Moving as fast as they could up the steep incline, they
reached Jake lying face down in the rocks.

"Jake's dead," Clark Sampson said. He rolled him onto
his back and felt for a pulse in his neck. "Let's catch the
mules."

The lieutenant quickly caught two horses and tied one
to an aspen tree. The tall miner caught three mules and led
them back at a jog; then he saw Jimmy! He made no attempt
to secure the mules, but dove for cover in the ravine and
carefully peeked around a rock. He couldn't see him. "He
was standing in the trail not ten seconds ago," he thought.
The tall miner pushed his rifle in front of him down the
rocky dry stream bed, stopping every few feet to peer over

the rim. Jimmy threw a rock across the ravine. The miner heard a sound of sliding rocks twenty yards to his left. He jerked his rifle toward the sound and waited. Again, the sound. The miner fired. Nothing. Except the echo of his own rifle shot.

"You get him?" called the lieutenant.

The miner heard the lieutenant's question, but was afraid to answer. He squeezed closer to a rock, tried to make himself small, held his breath for fear of being heard, but the roar of his own heart beating in his ear as he pressed against the rock unnerved him, and he raised his head for a peek over the rock.

"Bushwhacker," came from the rocks to his right. The miner rolled toward the sound and died. The heavy Spencer slug had torn through him and into the roots of a withering sagebrush.

"I can't catch the mules, Harry!" said the lieutenant, handing him a canteen. "Drink this while I go get the miner's rifle."

"Did you see him?" Harry asked. He was worried.

"No," Lieutenant Sampson answered.

"He's crazy! I'm getting out of here!"

"You wouldn't make it five hundred yards," Clark said simply. "You've had a long night, but you get your wits about you or you're not going to make it, pard!" Grabbing Harry by the shoulder, he gave him a light shake. "Savvy?"

Harry gamely tried to smile, his face contorted with fear.

"Riders coming in!" Sampson said. "I can't make them out," he continued. He handed the glasses to Harry.

"It's Alfredo and the corporal!" He passed the glasses back to Clark.

"Well, I'll be damned!"

As they drew closer, the squeak of leather and the rhythmical grunting of the horses trying to stay in control down the steep incline grew louder. "Lieutenant; Harry," said the corporal, nodding greetings.

"I can't believe you're alive!" marveled Harry. "How in hell did you get out of that desert?"

"Walked day and night. Crossed the Oregon Trail. Stage picked us up. Enough of your bunch and Prescott's riding in and out of South Pass City to start a gold mine. It wasn't hard to figure out where you had to be. We heard the shots a while back," said the corporal.

"What happened to your mules?" Alfredo asked waving his hand toward the packstring.

"That man with the buffalo rifle. He's crazy!" Harry sputtered.

"We've got to have pack animals and panniers. These are worthless." He picked up the oak sawbucks with their missing straps. "Wolves even ate the latigos off the packsaddles. We'll need four sawbucks, too.

"We just lost six mules a while ago," Sampson informed them.

"We could sling some of the sacks on our saddles," suggested Harry.

"We tried that, remember?" commented the corporal. "You want to walk this time?" he glared at Harry.

"I want away from here!"

"We can't go into town with the gold, so we'll have to have mules or packhorses. There are four of us now and just one of him. We'll have to draw him out and finish it. I know he has some of the mules tied up in those hills," Clark pointed.

"I don't think we're going to draw that fellar anywhere," Harry stated.

"He has no reason to come to us," Alfredo explained.

"Unless we can find the mules," offered the corporal.

"You'll find him, all right. He'll have a mule staked out for bait," Harry answered quickly.

"You afraid of that man?" Alfredo prodded.

"You're God Damned right! He'll stick a piece of your liver on a rock and use it for bait if he has to!"

Alfredo looked at Harry with contempt. Then he looked at the corporal. "Let's flush him out, amigo." With that, he turned; the corporal followed.

The lieutenant and Harry watched the pair ride up the ravine. Finally, on top, they dropped out of sight behind some trees.

Several groves of aspen, like pencil lines up the ravines, were visible in the distance. "Four mules. He didn't try to hide them," said the corporal.

They rode their horses into the trees for a closer look. "The bastard. No packsaddles," Alfredo said, adjusting the focus on his field glasses. "He's got us covered," Alfredo continued. "He's probably in that finger of timber two hundred yards above the mules."

The corporal looked at Alfredo, who with a light touch of the reins wheeled his horse, and together they rode back down the hill. Harry and the lieutenant were removing the gold sacks and patching them as best they could.

"Found the mules. He has them tied out in the open all right; without packsaddles," reported the corporal.

"What did I tell you!" blurted Harry.

"We can rig at least two of these," said the lieutenant, sorting through the stack of saddles. "There are two more down below that might have some latigoes or cinches. Go take a look, Harry!"

They assembled three packsaddles. There were no pads, but they would improvise.

"Let's go!" Sampson said after they had all four mounted. Riding single file and about twenty yards apart, they were in no hurry. Within sight of the mules they dismounted and walked slowly, using their horses as shields. Then like a leather strap whacking against a flat rock, a bullet dropped

the lead horse, followed immediately by the booming sound
of the large caliber rifle as it echoed down the mountain.

"Whoa, damn you, whoa!" shouted the men angrily as
they tried to control the horses. Alfredo's horse, held by the
lead rope, pulled hard and half dragged the vaquero twenty
yards down the ravine before breaking free, then running,
riderless at full speed through the sagebrush.

The corporal freed his left foot from the stirrup and
lowered his hand to the lieutenant. Sampson vaulted behind
the cantle of the corporal's horse. "Let's get out of here!"
shouted the lieutenant.

Alfredo, running at half speed, slowed and turned, as
Harry rode at a gallop to pick him up. Together, the two
horses carried the four riders safely down the hill.

CHAPTER TWENTY-NINE

HOMBRE!

At the sound of the shot, Charles turned his horse to the right to be above them. He could see the mules tied at the edge of the clearing in the aspen, but couldn't see Jimmy. He dismounted and pulled his .44 Winchester from the boot and levered a round into the chamber. He unwrapped the strap of his field glasses from around the horn and walked to a clump of trees. He sat down and propped his elbows on his knees and glassed the draws below. He could see the dead mules and the gold sacks. No horses. He slowly scanned the horizon and back to the gold. Antelope two miles out in the flats. Back to the gold. Heat waves. Coyote slinking into the underbrush. Where are they? Not much cover. Several deep ravines. He couldn't find Jimmy's horse.

An hour passed. Midday sun created a mirage that field glasses were not necessary to see. Ravens were above the depression, circling. Quiet. No wind. Maybe they got Jimmy? He stood and stretched his sore muscles. He went back to his horse, removed his canteen and slung it on his shoulder. Walking back up the hill, he slipped into the next ravine to the south. This took him out below the gold and downstream. Again, he stopped and listened. Horses! Three hundred yards north and above the gold in another ravine. He still couldn't see them. He crawled up a crevice to look. Nothing. He dropped back down to the floor of the ravine and continued downhill. Cautiously, he watched the ravens.

"Hombre!"

Charles froze in his tracks.

"Looking for the gold?"

The voice was behind him. "How did I miss him? I glassed every clump of sage." Tensed, every hair on the back of his neck raised, he felt a rifle barrel at his back.

"Drop the rifle, please."

He let it fall.

"Now the pistol. With the left hand."

He still couldn't see him.

"Move!" said the voice, as the Mexican jammed the rifle barrel between Charles' shoulder blades. With the gun in his back they climbed a sand and sagebrush-covered slope and descended the wall of the depression. Below them, Alfredo saw Harry, the lieutenant, and the corporal, huddled around the gold. Harry, on horseback, saw the pair first.

"Okay!" Harry said loudly. "Good work, Alfredo! We'll play with a new deck," he smirked, dismounting from his horse. Harry uncoiled his rawhide, slipped the noose around Charles' ankle and then took two half hitches around the other. He grabbed the same aspen branch that Jimmy had used to tie Harry earlier and ordered, "Sit!"

He put the pole behind Charles' knees and forced Charles' elbows under the pole, in precisely the same manner that Jimmy had bound him. Harry tied his hands over his shins and to the pole. "Learned that from your friend," he simpered, jerking the rope smartly.

"He'll deliver those mules," said the lieutenant, matter of factly, "and the packsaddles!"

CHAPTER THIRTY

FOUR MULES. FOUR HORSES.

Her loose fitting shirt was getting in her way as she cut thick slices of potato into the sizzling grease. She kept pushing back a wisp of hair with the back of her hand. The bacon was about done in the other skillet. She lifted a piece and handed it to Jedediah. He took her wrist and pulled her to him. Soft and warm, he kissed her on the mouth.

"You stop that, or we'll never get off this river!" she smiled.

After breakfast, she scoured the skillets with sand, and shaved off a sliver of soap. She set the skillets back on the fire to heat the water, and then rinsed them clean in the river.

"We'll cut their tracks on the Sandy," Jedediah said after he had finished saddling the stock. "Six or seven hour ride." He bridled her horse and handed her the reins.

She liked the funny hat with the short visor. Made him look boyish. "He needs his hair trimmed. And those greasy buckskins! Such power in a man," she thought. She had never seen hands so strong, nor so gentle. She kicked her horse along to ride by his side.

He looked at her smile, "Happy?"

Her face turned to a grin, and she hunched her shoulders and drew her arms across her chest while a tingle went down her back.

"We'll give the horses a blow here. Step down and stretch your legs," Jedediah said holding her horse by the lead rope on the halter.

"Is this the river?" Amy asked. "It's not very big."

"This is the Little Sandy. Another eight miles," Jedediah said. "Are you getting tired?"

"I'm all right," Amy answered. "How many times have you been through here, Jedediah?"

"More than I care to count. Seems different every time. Used to be full of buffalo fifteen years ago. Look over there." He pointed down the river. "There's a small herd now. That's just about where the Little Sandy flows into the Sandy. We may have to go that far south to cut their trail."

"Jed, Indians!"

"They've been riding with us the past hour. Waskie's people. They're friendly. They're probably going to cross in front of us and stalk that herd. We'll wait here and let them pass."

It was a small hunting party of eight braves. They raised the sign of the buffalo as they splashed across the Little Sandy on their way south.

He handed her a piece of jerky as they sat watching the Indians as they scurried up the river-bank. "Hold it in your mouth before you chew it."

She smiled. She had been eating the stuff for days. She would help him get to know her. "Wouldn't he be something at a ball in New Orleans. He would 'Yes, ma'am' all the ladies and have them crushing him with affection. Knows this country like his own hand. Maybe he won't leave it?"

The thought made her heart race and seem to catch in her throat.

"Jedediah, have you ever been to New Orleans?"

"No, ma'am."

"No, ma'am!" she heard and then thought, "Now he's getting serious. Got his mind on these fool tracks. Probably dreams about buffalo and tracks! I don't think he even cares about the gold. All that gold I've got in the bank wouldn't impress him either. He'd probably throw it in the river and head upstream."

"Let's go!" Jedediah said.

He started across the river without waiting for her. The Little Sandy had only two or three inches of water in it. The sagebrush, as high as the bottom of the stirrup, was still not tall enough to hide the column of dust Jedediah's and Amy's horses made as they traveled across the plain.

"We'll swing left and look for tracks."

"I thought that was what we were doing!" she complained.

He smiled but didn't answer. After a long pause he wondered, "Why did you ask?"

"Why did I ask what?" she pouted.

"If I'd ever been to New Orleans?"

"Oh, I just wondered."

Jedediah bent forward in the saddle to look closely at the trail in front of him. "Tracks all up and down the river; but they went up stream."

He had the animals in a trot most of the time. He was getting apprehensive. "Ravens." He pointed. "There!" They headed straight toward them. He tied the packstring in the ravine.

"You come with me," Jedediah said, starting up the hill. He half ran, with Amy close behind. The stench was powerful. Small animals and insects were everywhere. He found the remains of a human skeleton up the draw and two other mules down the ravine.

"Can you tell who the man was, Jedediah?" Amy asked slightly sick to her stomach.

"No, but he was killed with a tomahawk blow to the breastbone."

"Indians?"

"Or Jimmy."

"Any sign of Howard or Charles?" she asked. Worried, she continued, "Do you think they are still alive, Jedediah?"

"They made a stand below," he pointed, "Right where those two mules lie. Empty cartridge cases behind the carcasses. Up on the ridge, more cartridge cases. That would be the lieutenant or whoever's left. Someone shot the mules. They were tied up when he shot them. Whoever was behind those mules below was in a might of trouble. Their partner shot the mules to buy them time. Let's go up on that ridge."

"His horse was tied here," gestured Jedediah. The ground was scraped bare where the horse had trampled the sparse vegetation. They rode along the rim for twenty yards until he saw several small empty cartridge cases strewn about the hillside. Jedediah hastily dismounted, picked up a case and examined it. "Spencer," he said. "Jimmy was here. It must be four hundred yards across the canyon to the mules. Used his Sharps. That Jimmy's a good man."

Turning his horse to be downhill, he easily slipped into the saddle, and with a look at Amy said, "Someone took the gold out of here. If the tracks head for South Pass, it was Howard. If they're going downhill, it was the lieutenant. Let's go see."

They crossed two ravines up above, but saw no sign of horses. "Must be going down." They traversed the hill, still looking for tracks. Circling back, they picked up their mules as they started down the slope.

"Four mules. Four horses. I don't see any others," Jedediah said. "You hungry?"

Amy shook her head no and didn't speak. She fell farther

and farther behind as Jedediah's horse walked swiftly toward the west. From time to time he slowed and looked over his shoulder and waited for her to catch up. Then he turned off course and rode into a dry wash.

"We'll stop and rest awhile. You'll feel better with some coffee and fresh air," Jedediah said. He looked at her pale face and smiled and was again struck with her beauty.

"We going to camp here for the night?" Amy asked. She was tired and wasn't trying to hide it.

"No water," Jedediah said. "We'll ride a few more miles after we've rested. It's not too far to the Green."

"Oh!" she moaned. "I don't think I can get down, Jedediah.

He stepped up to her horse, and she fell into his arms. "I told you not to come." His voice was soft as she held him tightly. He had never felt anything like this before.

CHAPTER THIRTY-ONE

THAT BUFFALO GUN

The croaking cry of the raven was in synchrony with the painful pulsations in his temples. How long he had been unconscious was lost in the dimness of his struggle. His mouth was full of sand, and he couldn't see with his right eye. The three foot pole behind his knees dug against his flexed arms at the elbows. Blood soaked through his shirt where the bark had torn at the cloth. His wrists were tied together in front of his shins, and tied to the pole. Sometime during the night, when he had lost consciousness, his head was driven into the sand, and the pole kept him there. He tried to wiggle, but nothing worked! He tested his fingers and toes and a surge of gratitude welled in his chest; they moved! Unendurable pain was constant in his back and arms. The discomfort in his low abdomen was intense, and he was vaguely aware of his relief as he slipped into a stupor. The croaking reawakened him. It sounded strangely like his name. "Krock! Krock! Krock!" it sounded. He could hear voices at a distance and drawing nearer. He turned with a sudden rush onto his back. Water poured over his head; he could see!

"Your partner is coming to barter," said Harry. "We want you to look your best."

He tried to talk; words wouldn't come; he moved his lips to form the words; but nothing sounded. Try as he might, he could not speak! But he could hear:

"You want some water, do you?" Harry hissed.

"Give him a drink, amigo!" intoned Alfredo with authority.

Harry looked at him, blankly. Alfredo tore the canteen from his hand and tipped it to Charles' lips. Charles gratefully gulped huge swallows of water, choked and nodded his thanks to Alfredo. From his almost upside down position he could see the rider coming down the slope. It was Jimmy, with packsaddles on all four mules. He was leading a horse for Charles. He carried his Spencer over the pommel. At one hundred yards he stopped and dismounted. He did not go closer.

"Turn the mules loose and we'll release him, shouted the lieutenant.

"Untie him now," responded Jimmy. He cradled the Spencer in his arms and waited.

"Not until you release the mules!"

"No deal."

"Then we'll kill him!" Sampson said.

"Go ahead," Jimmy said, blandly.

"He's crazy!" Harry said.

"I'm not going to wait all day," Jimmy said. "Either shoot him or untie him. I'll hunt down every one of you sons of bitches either way!"

"Untie him, Harry!" ordered the lieutenant.

Harry cut the rawhide bonds with a long belt knife and then turned to look at the scout.

Charles rolled onto his back, stretched his legs to the fullest, turned to his abdomen, rested for a minute and slowly raised to his hands and knees. He looked about and stood, almost falling.

"Now what?" called Sampson, unsure of the next move.

"I want to see all four of you right beside my partner."

"Come on down, corporal," said the lieutenant, motioning to the ambusher on the hill.

"You move away from Charles; I'll move away from the mules," Jimmy said.

"Fair enough."

Jimmy tied the mules securely, next moved toward the ravine, leading two horses.

Charles could hardly walk, but gamely struggled up the incline, his legs not wanting to move. They made the exchange. Jimmy helped his partner into the saddle and said, "Hang on a few more minutes, pard, until we get back to my camp." He handed the reins up to him and said, "Can you make it?"

Forcing a smile Charles answered, "I feel much better already."

They disappeared over a ridge and then quickly traveled up the ravine and over a second ridge to Jimmy's camp.

"You get a little food and water down you and some rest and you'll be ready to ride!" said Jimmy, as he helped Charles out of the saddle. "That bunch will take an hour packing those mules. They won't be hard to trail."

The scout took the boot off the horn of his saddle and tied it onto the other saddle. He transferred the cartridge tubes in a similar manner. He picked up his Spencer and pushed it through the boot. "Seventy rounds in those Blakeslee tubes. Forty-two rounds in each of these boxes, and I've put one box in each saddle bag. You're back in business."

"Hell, there was a Deringer in my boot, but the way they had me tied I couldn't get to it! The frustrating thing was, I could touch the grips, but couldn't lift it!"

"You want to get a man's attention, tying him like they tied you is sure the way to do it," grinned Jimmy.

They finished a cup of coffee and doused the fire.

"You feel up to it?"

Charles stood and stretched to his full height, every muscle resisting painfully. "I'm ready."

Upon reaching the ridge where Jimmy had killed the mules, they stopped to search the sagebrush below.

"Two mile headstart." Handing the glasses to Charles, Jimmy asked, "They still together?"

"In a single file."

Both knew the four would separate. Jimmy unwound one canteen and handed it to Charles. "Two are going upriver. Probably through Union Pass. The other two are riding south." He looked at his friend and did not speak.

"Good luck," Charles said.

"Here," Jim said, handing him a small sack from his saddle bag. "Jerky. Keep your strength up," he smiled, and kicked his horse north along the Seeds-kee-dee.

The corporal and the lieutenant were making good time leading one pack mule apiece. From time to time they looked over their shoulders to see what the two riders following them would do.

"Looks like that Charles fellow is going south," said the corporal, "and that Buffalo Gun is coming after us!" They turned back upstream at a fast pace, with the loose ends of the mules' pack ropes flying wildly.

In the distance, Jimmy had patiently held his horse at a pace that slowly closed the gap. Each time the lieutenant stopped, Sampson saw the interval shorten.

"He's gaining on us!" shouted the corporal. "Shall we stop and fight him here, lieutenant?"

"Not yet."

Just below Union Pass is where that great river turns south in its long journey to the Colorado. In those upper reaches, Jimmy's father used to trap beaver and frolic at rendezvous along Horse Creek. Tom Fitzpatrick had named that creek in 1824, and the mountain men held a rendezvous in 1833 along those banks for the purpose of resupply for the coming beaver hunt, games, whiskey drinking, general hell raising and telling lies.

The big bay felt good and wanted to run, but Jimmy reined him to a ground eating trot that closed the distance to just a half-mile. He saw the riders ahead, nervously looking over their shoulders.

The ambushers sat on their ponies and watched the scout draw closer. "You go on upstream," said Sampson, "while I cross here." The lieutenant lashed his horse toward the river.

"I'll slow him down while you're in the water," called the corporal after the fleeing lieutenant. He tied his horse and mule and took cover.

The river was deep and could not be waded, so the lieutenant searched along the steep sagebrush-covered bank for an approach. Then through a gully that sloped to the water's edge, he jumped his horse into the fast stream and was almost pulled out of the saddle as the mule reluctantly followed. His horse was having great difficulty, so he slipped out of the saddle but lost the mule's lead rope in the process. He held on to the horn and the struggling horse carried him across. The mule reached the bank thirty yards below him.

A few minutes later, up the river, the bullet dropped twenty yards short, but Jimmy continued forward until he reached the shelter of a willow thicket. Six hundred yards away and across the river the mule lunged up the bank and then stood looking back across the river.

Using the brush as a screen, Jimmy walked his horse toward the corporal. A tributary creek offered protection at a diagonal away from the river. Now he had about four hundred yards to go. He left his horse and continued afoot up the creek for a hundred yards, crawled to the summit of the low ridge and looked for the corporal. It was farther than he thought. Five hundred yards! He opened the action of the Sharps and pushed in a linen cartridge. After closing the slant breech, the linen burst, exposing the black powder. He placed a primer and cocked the hammer. The heavy bullet nicked the stock of the corporal's carbine. Startled, the corporal ran to his horse and pulled the mule up the trail. The scout fired one more shot at the moving target and then bounded down the hill, through the sagebrush.

He saw the lieutenant moving through the trees across the river. The ground was uneven, but Jimmy let his horse have his head. The packmule could not keep up. The corporal would have to decide soon. The pack was starting to slip and the mule was not going to be a part of this race. The corporal dropped the lead rope and turned up a draw for cover. He left the saddle on the run and scurried behind a rock.

Jim dropped to the ground and placed the reins under his right knee. He picked out a rock at the horse's feet and fired. Fragments of gravel sent the horse fleeing through the sagebrush.

Jimmy led his horse at a jog back toward the river and then mounted it. He had come out above the corporal at a point two-hundred yards away. The corporal was lying behind the rock but fully exposed to the scout. Jimmy quietly advanced afoot toward the corporal, and when he was less than fifty-yards away, he called, "Bushwhacker! Where's your Gatling Gun?"

Taken by surprise, the corporal dove to the other side of the rock and out of sight. Jimmy checked the primers on his .44 Dragoon, cradled his Sharps and walked toward the rock.

The corporal jumped up abruptly, looked at the scout's Sharps, threw his carbine forcefully against the rock, and waited. Jimmy carefully laid his Sharps on the ground and continued to narrow the distance. He carried the big Dragoon with its muzzle pointed to the ground.

The soldier carried his .44 Colt crossdraw in a flap holster. He knew he could not beat the Dragoon. At twenty feet the scout stopped. He stuck the heavy .44 in his belt, peered intently at the corporal, and waited. The soldier's pistol was out of the holster when the heavy slug struck his chest. Jimmy, with a brief look of sadness on his face, walked closer to the man for a look at his enemy. Jimmy thought, "Damn waste of talent. This corporal was dedicated to his lieutenant, I'll say that for him." Turning he saw the mule standing patiently with the pack under his belly. Jimmy unhooked the cinch and let the pack fall to the ground. He tied the mule to a tree and patted his neck. "Damned horse would have kicked himself to death trying to get away from that pack," he thought. He walked back for his rifle and then up the hill to his horse.

The horse neighed softly upon his return. Jim tightened the cinch and mounted the bay, reined him toward the river where he took his saddle bags off and held them over the horn, coaxed his horse into the water, and the horse towed him across after he slipped out of the saddle. Once on the opposite bank he pulled the charges in his Dragoon and reloaded with skin cartridges and put fresh primers on the nipples. He reloaded his Sharps and carried it across the pommel.

"He's going to quit the river," Jimmy thought, "Heading into the mountains. It's ten miles before he'll reach the heavy trees. Better catch him now!" He kicked his horse to a gallop. He could see the lieutenant's dust trail ahead. Six hundred yards. "He's worried now." He watched Sampson let the mule go and ride for a ridge.

Just before reaching the summit, the lieutenant stopped his horse and pulled his Henry from the boot. His horse wouldn't stand still. He tried to align his sights. Impossible.

He increased pressure on the trigger and finally eased off. He started his squeeze again and fired.

At that instant Jimmy leaned flat against the horse's neck. Another shot dropped short. The ricochet whined dangerously close. Jimmy continued to let the bay run at full speed. His Sharps, clutched tightly in his right hand, was extended alongside the horse's head.

Up the hill, Sampson fired as fast as he could lever a round into the chamber. The lieutenant jerked his horse around and bounded over the rim with Jimmy two hundred yards below him. Sampson stopped at the bottom of the hill, dismounted, held the reins in his hand, kneeled with his rifle, sighted along the barrel of his Henry and waited the charge.

A moment later the scout topped the hill at full speed. The sound of the solid smack echoed down the slope as Jimmy plunged over his horse's head.

Down the slope, Sampson threw his leg over the horse, used the barrel of his rifle to slap the mount to a gallop.

At the crest of the hill, Jimmy's bay horse was dead. Jimmy had hit the ground with a roll and come up with his rifle. He swung his sights to the rider and led him one length, and fired. The lieutenant's horse, riderless, veered to the left and continued at a gallop. Jimmy watched for several minutes. Finally, he went back for his saddle bags and canteen. His bay had broken his neck during the fall. He walked down the hill to where the lieutenant lay dead. He found a gnarled stump of sagebrush, scooped out a shallow grave for the outlaw and buried him. He slung the saddle bags and canteen over his shoulder, picked up his his rifle, stared up the hill where his horse lay and started the long walk to the river.

Somewhere, below in the flats, among a rich stand of wheatgrass and wildrye, the mule had watched the approaching man. Finally, as the man drew nearer, the mule returned to grazing.

CHAPTER THIRTY-TWO

A BEAVER HOUSE

"A man doesn't get a second chance very often," thought Charles. "I must really be slipping to let them get the drop on me like that. I've been in many difficult situations, but never like last night!"

The memory of the grueling experience that had nearly cost him his life was haunting him as his horse cantered through the rolling sagebrush plains bordering the river.

"I'm riding a horse that's probably stolen," he thought, "and the rifle I have belongs to my friend. That just about sums it up. Gambling for a living, if you can call it that. Right now I don't even own a deck of cards. Why in the hell would a man risk his life chasing a rag-tag bunch of murdering thieves?" He watched his horse's bobbing head and continued, "I hit a winning streak; I'm living high, new suits, new boots; plenty of whiskey, and all the women I want. But then I lose it," he thought. "Just like that fancy new Sharps rifle I bought in Laramie City. Hell, I didn't even get to shoot it!" He chuckled to himself. "When I get back to the States,

I'm going to go into business like Howie, and find me a girl like the one that's got us chasing all over this Wyoming Territory."

His horse had begun to tire and wanted to walk. "He is a fine horse," Charles thought. "A gelding. Eleven hundred pounds, buckskin, mousy colored; the Mexicans call a grulla. I guess he's mine now. As much as I like horses, I ought to raise them, maybe even out in this wild country. The grass in this country is very nourishing." The horse had almost lulled him to sleep.

"I'd better start paying attention," he thought, "before this pair sets me up again. That Harry's not much, but that Alfredo is one tough hombre."

It was easy following the dust trail as he continued to get closer to the pair. Alfredo had pulled out in front of Harry by half a mile.

Now mules are one of the world's finest animals. They can pack half again as much as a horse and have more sense than most men, but trying to stay ahead of a well mounted pursuing rider without pack animals is most difficult. Harry's horse, lathered badly, started to blow. He coughed in more and more frequent intervals and wanted to stop in spite of Harry's flogging. He stopped. Bloody froth flecked the sagebrush as the horse coughed persistently and stood, legs wide apart, not moving, his sides and flanks heaving. Harry looked back at his pursuer and dismounted, frantically unlashing the packsaddle with its gold. He lifted each pannier off the sawbucks and dropped them to the ground. With a herculean tug he pulled the tongue of the buckle free from the hole in the latigo and threw the packsaddle down. Being free of the pack, the mule shook in a great shudder while Harry removed the bridle from his horse. With difficulty, he slipped the headstall over the mule's ears as he took the bit. Harry looked up at the approaching rider. He pulled his rifle from the saddle scabbard, mounted the mule bareback, and then headed straight for the river. Its steep bank offered cover for a stand. Upon reaching the river, Harry slowed the mule and jumped over the bank to the water's edge. He found a log and cowered behind it awaiting the rider. Nothing happened. He could neither hear nor see him. He scrambled up the bank for a look. "He's catching the mule! Too far away for a shot," he thought, but he tried. The rider below had heard the shot and fixed the position of his enemy.

Far away, Charles caught the mule and turned to walk him back to Harry's horse. It was six hundred yards to the river where Harry lay waiting, but the distance was too great for the limited effectiveness of the blunt nosed .44 rimfire cartridge. That .44 rimfire was a dandy one-hundred-yard cartridge, but to hit anything at six-hundred yards was pure luck.

At the river, Harry lay, covered with mud, his rifle pointed at his adversary. Holding slightly over to allow for the bullet drop, he fired. Way low! He increased the elevation. Still low. He fired many times.

The bullets dropped harmlessly around Charles as he dismounted from his horse and tied the mule. Afterwards he unsaddled Harry's horse. The pony heaved with stridorous breathing while blood streamed from his mouth and nose. Then he fell down.

The grulla munched grass when Charles picked up his reins and tied him fast with a halter rope. He unloosened his cinch and said aloud, "No need his shooting you, horse."

He jacked a round into the chamber of the Spencer and slung the cartridge box across his chest as he turned to the river.

To the west of the Green the low range of foothills was backed by a pine covered expanse of mountain ranges of varying height, without the towering peaks of the Wind

River Range that stood on the east side of the Seeds-kee-dee. Ham's fork started its descent from wild strawberry-covered hillsides twenty-five miles toward sundown. But here on the banks of this beaver stream the sagebrush grew right to its edge. This tought, deep-rooted plant of the western high plains offered shelter to small animals and food for large fauna; birds nested in the tangle of dense vegetation and the prairie chicken hid from the soaring hawk.

When Harry had jumped over the bank and half fallen to the water's edge below, he had thrown himself behind the log and desperately begun digging the wet sand with the stock of his rifle; then he abandoned his rifle and used his hands. After taking the shots at the hopeless target, he had settled down to survey his untenable position. His back to the river, a steep bank immediately in front of him and ample draws, shallow depressions and heavy sagebrush to afford cover for his enemy, he crawled up the incline to take a look. He couldn't see him. He saw the horses and the pack-mule. "He could be in any one of those gullies," he thought. He laid his rifle on a rock and tried to move the log. It wouldn't budge. He sat down with his back against the bank and pushed the log free with his legs. He picked up his rifle and waded into the river pushing the log in front of him. He couldn't hold his pistol and his rifle out of the water and at the same time hold onto the log, but he tried. The log was slippery and wanted to roll. He had dropped his pistol but held the rifle as the current carried him downstream.

Now Charles reached the river-bank in time to see Harry crawling up the opposite side. He took a snap shot at one-hundred-yards and missed. Charles Richfield jogged up the stream, and then waded into the river and rolled onto his side holding his rifle out of the water as he swam across. He rested a few minutes to let his pulse return to

normal and then started walking slowly down the river.
A smack on the water startled him as he swung his rifle to
the left and dropped to one knee. Beaver! He stopped and
then continued his slow walk, drifting to his right to check
the gullies and then back to the river. Nothing. Slowly
descending the cut bank, he peered up and down the river.
Not a sign.

Presently Charles searched the willow thickets and brush
piles without success. He swam the river to pick up his horses.
"Can't take you with me ole boy," he said aloud, as he
inspected Harry's horse. "You're looking better though,"
he thought. "With good water and grass, you'll be as good
as new in a couple of days. That is, if the wolves don't get
you tonight. An Indian will have you in his string in a
fortnight. I'll lead you down river so the ambusher won't
find you."

Deliberately Charles Richfield took his time packing the
gold onto the mule and next tightened the cinch on his
saddle. "You ready, boy?" he said aloud to the trembling
horse. He led the three animals at a slow walk toward the river.

Conversely Harry had no horse and his ammunition was
useless. He tried to fire at the swimming enemy, but the
powder was wet. He turned down the river for shelter. A
beaver house! Covered by mud and earth, sticks protruded
in a tangled morass. "I'll find the passageway," he thought.
"There it is!" He clutched his rifle in a panicking rage, held
his breath and submerged to enter the den. His rifle lodged!
He tried to retreat, but he was caught fast. His chest burst
with pain for want of air as he released his grip. "I must
have air!" But there was only water.

The late afternoon passed while Charles took several
minutes to walk the six hundred yards to the river for one
last look. On the opposite bank, he saw a beaver house,
overgrown with willows, with gray and white sun-bleached
sticks protruding from its roof; those sticks appeared as if

the bones of some large prehistoric animal strained to reach the surface of the earth.

"Probably found the entryway," he thought. He looked at the sun, fiery red on the horizon. "My friends will be needing me," he thought, as he turned to walk down the river.

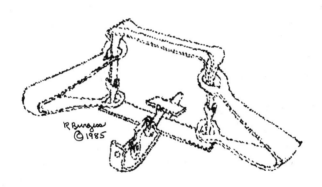

CHAPTER THIRTY-THREE

"HOWIE"

"I can go down to the kitchen, Lillian! You don't have to go to all this bother."

"Howard, you eat your breakfast! Then I'll change that dressing."

"Doc Jackson said he would be over this morning."

"Doc Jackson told me to change it. He had to go up to the mine."

"Elk steaks, biscuits, gravy and fried potatoes. That would give a man an appetite," said Howie, looking over the large tray. "You know, Lillian . . . about last night. I couldn't control myself."

Color rushed to her cheeks. "You are a big, strong man, Howie. I felt so bad about your wound. You looked so helpless."

He smiled a sheepish smile. "Is that all?"

"I have cared about you, Howard. You should not have been chasing around the desert after all those thieves!"

"She is a beautiful woman," he thought. "I didn't know

she liked me this much. I gave her the job of running this hotel a year ago, and now she has fallen in love with me."

He spoke seriously, "Somebody has to catch them. It's getting so I can't send a wagon out without trouble. A man has got to protect his property!" he said.

Lillian continued to busy herself about the room without speaking.

"Miss Stafford was coming to marry me."

"Do you love her?" Lillian could not bring herself to look at Howard.

"I thought I did. It may have been New Orleans. And all the excitement. She owned a gambling casino. And all that gold!"

Lillian blurted, upset, "I watch these miners every day. They sell everything they owned and leave their wives and families to come out here and kick around a bunch of rocks!" she said heatedly.

"Why did you come to South Pass, Lillian?"

She turned reflective. "My husband was killed in the war. There was nothing for me in Indiana. I had an opportunity to go West to Oregon. This is as far as I got!" She didn't continue, but rolled and unrolled the bandage with her nervous remembering.

"Better change this dressing before you wear those out," he said with a smile.

"Your arm is purple looking, but it's not swollen. It looks clean, too. A few more days, and it will be healed."

Howard looked at his arm and turned his hand over. "Then I'll have to get back after that gold. Hell, they're probably half way to San Francisco by now." He opened and closed his fingers. "So far, we haven't recovered a single sack of the stuff!"

Lillian, pacing the floor nervously said, "Howie, you won't be mad at me?"

He looked at her quizzically and didn't answer.

"Promise?"

Not knowing what to expect, he simply shrugged his shoulders.

She hesitated, not knowing where to start, took a deep breath and said, "Miss Stafford spent several days in this hotel. She had the opportunity to take a stage almost every day. She seemed very friendly with that fellow they call Harry. They were in the back room together at the Black Horse. When I saw they were going on the same stage, I got worried. I tried to wire you at End of Track but couldn't reach you." She continued her nervous pacing.

"Won't you sit down, Lillian? You were going to wire me that they were friends?"

"No, I was going to tell you what I had done."

"And that was what?"

"Well," she smiled weakly, "each of those forty pound sacks has only ten pounds of gold in the top. I had the boys fill a sack with thirty pounds of sand for the bottom."

"You mean we've been chasing seven hundred pounds of sand around in that God damned desert?" he yelled.

"Howie," she purred, tracing her index finger around his bare chest, "the rest of the gold is under the bed."

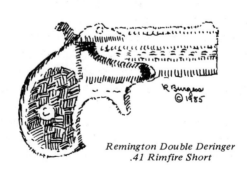

Remington Double Deringer
.41 Rimfire Short

CHAPTER THIRTY-FOUR

AMY'S GOLD

Jedediah, bent low to the ground, straightened in the fading light and said in a low voice, "Two riders picked them up here." He pointed to several sets of tracks.

"But there should be three of them!" Amy said. "Are you sure?"

"Looks like just two," he repeated. Worried, he urged her, "Come on. We'll never make it to the Green by dark!" With a flip of the reins and a tug of the lead rope Jedediah headed the column toward sundown.

"Here's where they split. Two went north, two south." Following one set of tracks a short way, he stopped and turned in the saddle. "Our boys went with them."

Catching up with him, Amy said, "I'm holding you up, Jedediah. You go on ahead. I'll follow your trail."

He ignored her remark. "It will be dark soon. They are not very far ahead of us. We can't help them both. Upstream? he asked, "or downstream?"

Her face lit up briefly. "Downstream."

He turned to glass ahead. "Not even a dust trail. We'll go straight south until dark, and then back west to the river. We'll cut off several miles.

An hour passed and the sun was lower when they heard rifle shots from upriver. The pair looked at each other, and continued south. More muffled shots came from upriver.

"Our man's still alive!"

At sunset they paused to rest the horses. Amy didn't want to get out of the saddle, but her knees hurt. "There haven't been any shots downriver, Jed." She looked at him, her face pinched.

"Probably won't be this late."

The outline of the mountain range changed rapidly from blue, to purple, to black. The indistinct ridges, with their sage-filled valleys, melded with the sand-muffled sounds of the horses' feet. They continued to bear to the southwest as darkness surrounded them. Amy could hear but could not see the mule in front of her. She wished Jed would stop but knew he would not. "He wants to get around them. If I weren't along, he'd ride all night," she thought.

The stars were out now, and her eyes had become accustomed to the dimness. She could make out Jedediah ahead from time to time. The temperature had dropped, and a blanket of cold air sent a chill down her back. She wished she had a wrap for her shoulders. The cadence of her horse's stride was soothing. Her head relaxed to the methodical plodding of her horse's gait. "Jedediah will warm me. Jedediah will warm me. Jedediah will warm me. Jedediah will . . ."

"You all right?" His hand was on her shoulder.

She awakened with a start. "Oh. Huh?"

"You asleep? We've stopped to water the horses. Can you hold on for another hour?"

"I'm doing fine. I'm cold!" she pouted.

He untied his wool coat from behind the cantle and gave it to her. "Don't fall out of the saddle!"

They continued into the darkness at the rhythm of the packstring. Try as she might she could not stay awake.

"We'll stop here," he said, helping her out of the saddle.

"I'll get these packs off the mules. You hungry?"

"No."

"Look through these panniers and find the blankets while I grain the horses. I'll build a fire in a minute."

She stacked the blankets and sat on them until he returned.

"I'll help you roll these out," he said. "Lie down and I'll cover you up." Pulling two wool blankets up to her chin he noticed that she was already asleep!

He started a small fire and fed it with branches of sagebrush. The horses pawed the ground for more grain when he removed their nosebags. "In three hours I'll give you some more," he said aloud.

Returning to the fire, he pulled off his boots and slipped under the blankets. He lay there, feeling her softness and realized how lucky he was to find such a woman in this vast and violent wilderness. "What will she do when we decide this hand? The last card should be dealt tomorrow." She was sound asleep but cuddled against him for warmth.

"First light in an hour," he said. He was standing above her and gently nudged her with the toe of his boot.

"Um."

"Horses are saddled. Nothing left but these blankets. Come on, let's go!"

"Jedediah!" she said in a teasing manner.

"Here are your boots. I'll help you!"

"Come back to bed."

"Woman, it's getting light!"

"Um huh," Amy said, slipping her hand from under the blanket and curling her fingers.

The stars were still out when the rested horses started their ground eating pace. Light in the east was coming fast. It was cold. She wore Jedediah's heavy coat this time. The sleeves were much too long, but they felt so warm! He had kept a blanket out of the pack for his shoulders and later tied it behind the saddle as it warmed up at sunrise. She rode up beside him.

"Don't you ever dream of a souffle?" she asked.

"Huh?"

"Or an omelet?"

"You hungry?"

"Yes!"

He reached into his saddlebag. Here's some jerky. And . . ."

"Don't chew it," she chimed in with a laugh. "Just hold it in your mouth!"

Jedediah scanned the ridges ahead of him for an hour, and from time to time he stopped to look upriver for several minutes. He could see deer, elk and buffalo leaving the river bottom from their morning water. Antelope were everywhere.

"There!"

"What is it?" Amy whispered.

"Rider. Leading a mule. That's one of them!" Dropping the field glasses from his eyes, he urged, "Back down in the draw!" Out of sight he continued, "I don't believe he saw us."

He tied the four mules to snags of brush in the ravine and said, "This shotgun is made ready by cocking the hammers and pulling one trigger then the other. Understand?" he asked looking straight into her eyes.

She nodded her head "yes", excited and apprehensive.

"You stay right here!"

"Jedediah! I love you!"

Blushing to his ears, he said, "Girl, you have the darndest timing!" He wheeled his horse up the bank and out on top. "Damn! He saw us. He's heading for the river!" he said aloud to himself.

At this moment up the river Alfredo turned and fired from the saddle. The rifle bullet whined dangerously close to Jedediah who pulled his horse to a stop. Jedediah would have to approach from a different direction. He turned his horse into a ravine heading to the water's edge. Out of sight, he kicked his horse to a gallop and rode up on the ridge.

Several minutes passed while Alfredo decided what to do. He jumped his horse and mule into the river and was half way across when they got in trouble. The horse went under, and the mule got tangled up with his pack and the saddle of Alfredo's horse. They both went under water, fighting frantically. Alfredo swam to the opposite shore.

Far below, Jedediah swam his horse across keeping his rifle and saddlebags high and dry. Upon reaching the bank, a quick inspection of his rifle showed it free of water. Fifty yards upriver, Alfredo, horseless, stood watching. Jedediah slowly rode toward him.

Alfredo's rifle was lost. Maybe it was on his horse, but he checked the loads in his pistol. Useless! Wet! He stood on the river bank, waiting. The approaching rider, his rifle cradled in his arms, drew nearer.

Jedediah stopped a few feet from his enemy, dropped the reins around the horn of the saddle and slowly swung the muzzle of the rifle until it pointed at the vaquero's chest.

Alfredo drew his bowie knife and crouched, made a gutteral sound low in his throat, and squinted his dark glistening eyes. They faced each other a full minute without speaking. Jedediah slowly straightened to his full height in the saddle, lightly touched the rein of the horse and pivoted him down the river.

After two hundred yards Jedediah saw her swimming her horse and leading one mule. In the middle of the stream the mule pulled the lead rope out of her hand and turned to swim with the current. She reached the west shore, raced down the bank to the mule and jumped her horse into the river. "She's going back!" he realized. The mule turned to the east bank with Amy and her horse close behind.

Jedediah, at a full gallop, entered the river after her. He reached the other side shortly after she did.

"Oh, Jedediah, I thought you were dead!"

"Where were you going?"

"I had to know! I heard the shots!"

"What did you do with the shotgun? You didn't even have a gun!"

"I left it with the mules."

She was thoroughly soaked and without a hat.

"Were you going to swim those mules across one at a time?"

"I'm wet."

"You would have drowned every one of them. And yourself!"

"I'm cold, Jedediah."

"I told you to stay with the mules!"

"Jedediah, I'm cold."

"You will have to stay with me!" he said firmly.

"I'm shaking. I can't control it, Jedediah," she said, her voice trembling. "Hold me! Take me home," she whispered, drawing near him.

"Amy . . . Amy . . ."

"You can say it, Jedediah," she said, gently.

"I love you."

CHAPTER THIRTY-FIVE

1868

It was an early fall that year. Beaver had cut aspen limbs along the stream, dragged them to the bank, dove to the bottom of a deep hole, carefully buried the butt-end of each limb deeply into the mud of the feed-pile and surfaced, surrounded by golden aspen leaves. The current carried the leaves, swirling, against a partially submerged log.

Jimmy Lee Robineaux jumped the small stream, and walked up to the mule, grazing, its head down, unconcerned for the man. The mule's pack, lashed securely with a diamond hitch, contained its load of gold. Jimmy picked up the mule's lead rope and walked down the river.

In the early evening Jimmy saw Charles riding his horse, and leading two pack-mules up the river straight toward him. When they were a few yards apart, they greeted each other.

"Charles, I see you're well," said Jimmy.

"I'm fine, Jimmy."

"Have you seen Jedediah and the girl?" asked Jim.

"Yes. A couple of hours ago. They're on their way to

South Pass. I told them I'd find you and that we'd meet them in South Pass City."

"Be dark in an hour. Let's camp here for the night," said Jimmy.

In the dull evening light, the two men unloaded the mules, and ran their picket line. From Charles' saddle bag, they were able to prepare a modest meal. A bottle of brandy helped fortify the coffee.

They told each other the story of the day's events. Jimmy said, "My saddle is still up on the hill." He pointed westward. "We can repack the gold on two mules. I'll ride the other. Howie will be happy to recover these packs."

"Have you checked those sacks?" He saw the quizzical look on Jimmy's face. "Hell, it's mostly sand!"

A big grin spread across Jimmy's face, and he couldn't hold back the laughter. "You're kidding me!"

"No, I'm not. There's a little gold in the top of each sack, and the rest is sand!" Charles poured some more brandy into Jimmy's cup. "But you should see the way Miss Amy looks at Jedediah with those big brown eyes of hers. She's the one who's found the gold!"

THE END